I0578112

# PRINCE'S MISSION

## FREELANCER 2

## JANE KILLICK

Elly Books

# Chapter One

I RESTED MY HEAD on the warm, naked chest of my prince and listened to the thumping of his heart after sex. The smell of him – the smell of *us* – filled the royal bedchamber with a steamy musk which would alert the staff to what we had been doing long after I had sneaked out of Londos House. It was illicit sex, it was exciting: he was the second in line to the Fertillan throne and I was a lowly spaceship captain – it was part of the thrill. But it was also the barrier that kept us apart for long, lonely periods and reduced our relationship to moments snatched in secret.

"I have to go, Stephen," I said as I drew my index finger across his chest and traced a line through the hairs still damp with sweat.

He clasped my hand. "Don't go, Cassy," he said.

"I have to. We have a cargo run."

"Anywhere interesting?"

"Leontes Station. It's where Keya and some of the scientists went after the Octavia Research Station was destroyed."

The mention of it still sent a wave of guilt through my body. The survivors had thanked us for giving them the chance to get out before the station exploded, but the truth was if I hadn't gone there in the first place, the station would still exist, intact, spinning in space with scientists living on board and carrying out their work.

"How long will you be gone?"

"Not long. A week, possibly. It's a return trip. We take them a shipment of supplies and we bring back a shipment of fertiliser."

"They make fertiliser there?" said Stephen. "I thought it was a research station."

"Everyone makes fertiliser." I giggled. "It's what happens to your food after you've eaten it."

"Ah." He nodded, as if he should have known. "You're bringing back their waste. Delightful."

"It's not that bad. By the time it gets to us, it's no more than dry granules. They extract all the water for recycling and what's left can be used on farms on Fertilla. You should know that, your family runs a farming planet."

"That's my brother's business," he said. "He won't tell me what he's up to, even when I ask."

"Then you'll have to take my word for it that it's a very important cargo of poo and I have to go." I slipped my hand from his grasp and slid away from his smooth, comforting body. But he pulled me back close again with his other hand.

"Stay a bit longer, Cassy," he whispered.

I moaned at his touch as my nipple sat up straight as if begging for more. I sighed at the knowledge that I could not obey what my body wanted. "I can't be late, Stephen. If I'm not there to load the supplies onto my ship, they might not hire me again."

Reluctantly, I prised myself away from him and stood naked at the end of his bed. I waited for a moment, enjoying the way he looked at me with raw desire, before I turned away and faced the pile of my clothes on the floor where we had thrown them towards a chair and missed.

The reality of the room where we'd had our illicit sex came into sharp focus. Back on my ship, my room had a chair moulded into a practical shape from cheap artificial materials, whereas the chair in Stephen's bedchamber was made from real wood varnished to a golden lustre that caught the light. Rifling for my underwear beside it, I became aware of the softness of the carpet under my bare feet. Climbing into my trousers, I estimated the large, ornate room was big enough to fit my own bedroom inside it four times over. Even the bed, with its imposing frame reaching to the ceiling, could sleep a whole family. Stephen, however, seemed to command it, as he lay with the sheets draped casually across his bottom half and watched me fasten the buttons of my shirt.

I stopped myself from clambering back into bed and resting my head on his exposed chest which had made such a sensual pillow only minutes before.

Dropping my gaze and bending down to attend to my boots, a shadow fell across me and I was aware of Stephen's presence. He had put on a robe of deep blue material that shimmered in the light. He offered his hand, I took it and he pulled me up to standing.

We faced each other and the smell of him again begged me to stay.

"I hate it when you go," he said.

"It's only for a week."

"A week this time, a month last time, who knows how long next time?"

"It's my job."

"I wish it wasn't."

"*Your* job doesn't make things any easier, Your Highness."

He looked away, uncomfortably. "Don't call me that. The staff call me that."

"If you were an ordinary person, I wouldn't have to sneak in here like some kind of thief."

"If we made our relationship official, my family would have certain expectations of you and you wouldn't like it."

"I don't think your family would like that I'm a lowly, freelan–"

He pulled me close before I could finish, and devoured my words with his lips. I returned the kiss, but he became distracted and pulled away.

There was a mischievousness in his eyes. For once, it wasn't motivated by sex. "Why don't you work for me?" he said.

"In the royal household?" The whole joy of my job was I wasn't tied to any one place. I was absolutely a freelancer, with the emphasis on *free*. "I'm not being your scullery maid, if that's what you're thinking."

"No," said Stephen. "I could hire you. You're a freelancer for hire, aren't you?"

"Yeah, but you already have your own spaceships and crews of Fertillan Guard."

"I need someone who I can trust who can operate in secret. My brother keeps wormholing off somewhere and I need to know why."

"I'm not spying on your brother!"

"Why not, Cassy? You could report back to me, it would give

us an excuse to see each other and I wouldn't have to worry about you going away on long, dangerous missions."

I put my hand to his shoulder and felt its warmth. It was tempting to think I could take a job which would allow me to see him more often, but the last time my boss and my lover had been the same person I was forced to watch his execution and stand helpless as his body was sent to burn in the nearest sun.

"Sharing a bed and business is never a good idea," I said.

"I'll pay a top rate."

"Money and sex are always tempting, Stephen, but…"

"It'll be an honest job for an honest fee," he said. "Like all your other jobs."

"But it won't be like my other jobs," I said. "I thought that was the point."

"Think about it, at least."

I had thought about it already, but I didn't want to leave him on a note of rejection. "Sure," I said. "I'll think about it."

I allowed my hand to fall away from his shoulder and walked across the plush carpet to the door. As I turned the handle, I considered looking back at him one final time, but our goodbyes had already taken too long and so I stepped through the doorway into the unwelcoming chill of the corridors of the royal household.

# CHAPTER TWO

MAKE AN ERROR travelling through a wormhole and it would kill you. Inject too much qubition into the Quantum Entanglement Drive and it could explode. Inject too little and the wormhole could become unstable. Choose to enter the wrong wormhole and it could spit you out in the middle of a sun or send you on a collision course with a planet.

Every time we engaged the QED and jumped to a different part of the Obsidian Rim, I relied on Freddi to make the calculations. The computer handled the mathematics, of course, but without Freddi's instincts I wouldn't want to risk my life. He had been living and working in space since I was a child. He was the only crew member I would ever need and he was my friend.

Freddi made the calculations for the jump to the Leontes system and I endured the physical pain of going through the wormhole because I knew we would come out safely on the other side.

When it spat us out into normal space, Freddi pushed back

the strands of his ginger and grey hair that had fallen over his face and gave me a satisfied smile.

I breathed deep – free from G-forces on my lungs – and checked the data on my screen. We were sitting in uninhabited space, a safe distance from Leontes' giant red sun and its single gaseous giant planet. An automatic identifying beacon confirmed that Leontes Station was in orbit around it.

"I'll send a message to say we're coming," said Freddi.

"Computer?" I called up to the ceiling. "What's the journey time to Leontes?"

"Twenty-three hours in normal space," said an unemotional, gender non-specific voice from the speakers above me.

"Thank you, computer." I sighed and remembered the old voice that once spoke to me from above. "I miss Ship."

'Ship' was the name we had given to the personality that used to belong to the ship's computer system. Although 'given' was perhaps overstating it. We had called her 'Ship' before we thought of a name and it sort of stuck.

"I miss her too," said Freddi. "I could bring her back if you want. Ship's voice and personality were a standard, commercially available model, so I could find the right one and activate that. It would be a new Ship, though, reset to baseline, without the memory of everything we've been through together."

"No," I said. "That would be disrespectful. Almost like raising the dead."

Ship's personality and memories had been purged after a man had hacked into her systems and set in motion a series of events which would have caused the engines to explode and all of us to die. The purge saved our lives, but we were not able to save Ship.

"We should get a new personality," I said.

Freddi nodded. "I've been thinking about that. I've looked at what's available and I think I've found something that will work. We should give the ship's computer a proper name this time."

"Yes. Something friendly and feminine."

"I was thinking I'd like to call her Ellen." He watched me closely and waited for my reaction.

"Your wife's name?"

"I thought it would be nice to have a little bit of her with me in space."

It had been many years since his wife died and I knew the memory of her death still haunted him. "Are you sure?"

"I've thought about it a lot."

If I had lost the love of my life, I wouldn't want to be reminded of it every time I spoke to the ship's computer. But I could see in his face that the tribute was important to him. "It's a good name."

He smiled. "I'll get on it."

"After we've conducted business on Leontes, let's sort the cargo, see Keya and then we can welcome a new computer."

"Yes, Captain."

We turned the ship around and lay in a course for Leontes Station.

"Course set," confirmed the computer from the speakers above. "All systems now on automatic."

The unemotional, gender non-specific tone of its voice grated on my ears. It would be good to have a real personality back running things again. I knew it was just a machine and its voice was merely a veneer, but when you travel through the vacuum of space, you need all the friends you can get.

THE GIANT METAL bay doors clanged and hissed as they parted and the seal was broken between our ship and the outside. A chink of light from Leontes Station filtered through the crack like a sun peering over the horizon of a planet, and fell on our faces. I squinted until the gap widened, the light was all around us and I could see out into the vast hangar. It seemed so empty, compared to the bustling space ports where we were used to docking, but there were several people milling about in overalls who looked like they worked there. One of them beckoned me over and told me where they wanted our freight to go, while Freddi went back into the relative gloom of the ship's hold to unclip the travel harness which had kept the stack of crates in place during transit.

When I returned, Freddi was already walking down the ramp, carrying one of the crates. He limped a little from the accident that broke his pelvis in his youth, but it didn't seem to hamper him. "Come on, Cassy," he said as he passed me. "The sooner we get this done, the sooner you can buy me a beer."

"I'm buying you a beer?" I said.

He dumped the crate a few metres from the ship and turned to me with a grin. "That's very good of you to offer."

"*One* beer." I picked up the next crate from the stack. "Then we've got another cargo to load up."

"Ah," said Freddi. "Moving poo. What a delightful job you've lined up for us."

I smiled as I carried my crate over to where Freddi had put his. It was damn heavy. About on the limit of what I could comfortably carry. I would be needing a beer myself after unloading the whole shipment.

It was after I had carried out the second crate that Keya came and found us. She stood at the edge of the hangar and waved to catch my attention.

She looked immaculate as always. She wore scientist whites of crisp and clean tunic and trousers, with neatly applied make-up which enhanced her features with subtle shades. There was a healthy colour about her complexion, and her smile, when she saw us, looked genuine.

"Cassy!" she said. She opened her arms and embraced me in a friendly hug. I hadn't expected her to do that, but allowed myself to soften into the warmth of her body.

Freddi put down the crate he was carrying and came to join us.

"Freddi! So good to see you." She hugged him and he stiffened until she let him go and he was able to relax.

"How are you, Keya?" I said.

She swayed her head from side to side as if she was unsure. "I live. I work."

"Leontes Station is working out for you?"

"The project I was working on was taken away from me just at the point I thought we were ready to begin clinical trials, so I was a bit upset about that. But I can't complain." There was sadness in her expression for a moment, before she forced it away with a smile. "Anyway, I didn't come down here to talk about that. I want to know all the gossip. What's going on with you and Stephen? Are you still together?"

"Every chance they get," said Freddi before I was able to answer.

I glared at him. He was so indelicate sometimes.

"That's good," said Keya. "I'm glad."

"Yeah," I said doubtfully.

"Not good?" suggested Keya.

I sighed. "It's difficult. He proposed that I work for him – you know, as a freelancer – so we could see each other more often."

"Really?" said Freddi. "You didn't tell me."

"Because I turned him down. It would be like being his paid mistress."

"Cassy…" Keya reached forward and took my hand. "You need to seize the opportunity for love when it comes your way. Take it from me."

She released my hand and, in the following moment when no one said anything, we all knew she was referring to her own lover: killed in the explosion that destroyed Octavia Research Station, along with many of her colleagues and all of her work.

"Anyway," she said, forcing away the moment with a smile. "It was good to see you again."

"Yeah," said Freddi.

"Thanks for giving us the work," I said.

"No problem." Keya waved us goodbye and went back into the main part of the station.

"How many more crates have we got to get out of the ship before we can go for that beer?" I asked Freddi.

"Uh… eight? Ten?"

I frowned.

"I'll make a start on those if you like," said Freddi. "You can go find where this poo is that they want us to take back."

"Right."

Freddi went back to the ship and I looked around for someone to ask. The man in overalls I had spoken to earlier was on the other side of the hangar, but I had barely taken a step before the sound of someone saying my name made me stop.

"Cassy?"

A man stepped out from behind a stack of crates. He was plump and balding with sunken blue eyes and looked as though the tunic he was wearing was too thick and warm for him because he had a sheen of sweat across his brow.

"It's Cassy, isn't it?"

"Yes," I said, warily.

"Remember me? I was on Octavia Research Station with Doctor Keya Sharma."

There were a lot of scientists dressed in the same white uniform back on that station. After so many of them died, I made an effort to forget almost all of them. "I'm sorry, I…"

"Doctor Muna Raymon." He held out his hand to shake, then apparently thought better of it. He pulled his hand back again and wiped his sweaty palm across his tunic. "Would you be interested in taking a passenger?"

"I can't do a passenger run at the moment. We have a shipment of freight to take back to Fertilla, sorry."

I side-stepped round him as I saw the man in overalls heading for the exit.

But Doctor Raymon hurried past me and stood in my way. "Fertilla would work," he said. "I don't want to work on a space station any more. After Octavia, I get palpitations, you know what I mean?"

"Not really," I said.

"I grew up on Prithvi. It's a planet. I don't know if you know it."

"Um…?"

"I need to be on a planet again. They're a lot more difficult to blow up, if you know what I mean."

"As I say, we've got this cargo run…"

"I can pay the going rate," he offered. "I'll be no trouble. Not many ships stop off here, you see, and I really want to leave."

I thought about it for a moment. It was free money for no extra work. "I suppose I could take you, but we're leaving in a few hours and you'll have to be ready by then."

"I can be ready," said Raymon. "I'll see you in a few hours."

He turned and rushed away, dodging between the crates in the hangar, and disappeared into the rest of the station.

I pulled out my P-tab and ran a security check on Doctor Muna Raymon. His story checked out, he was indeed a scientist from the planet Prithvi – an expert in molecular biology and virology, no less – and the image on his details matched the flustered man I had been talking to.

What I didn't do was stop to question why he was so flustered. Or why he had virtually ambushed me from behind a crate. Or why he was prepared to leave with only a few hours' notice.

On reflection, maybe I should have stopped to question. Perhaps then I would have realised how much of a bad idea it was to let him board my ship.

# CHAPTER THREE

I TOOK FIRST WATCH in the control room while my spaceship pulled away from the Leontes system on course for uninhabited space where we could fire up the QED. Once we were clear, I put all systems on automatic and went down to the engine room to find Freddi.

The engine room was a part of the ship I rarely set foot in. But, on those rare occasions, it always reminded me of the power at my command with the rumble of the engines that vibrated up through my feet and into my body. The last time I had been down there, it was to clean up the mess after the man who had tried to sabotage our computer received a well-deserved Energy Expenditure blast to the head. But although the blood had gone, the scars of our fight were still visible. Burns from EE weapons fire were seared into the walls and one was streaked across the control panel like a comet shooting past a starfield of green indicator lights.

The workstation which allowed access to the hardware for the ship's computer lay opposite. I rested my elbows on top of it and peered over to where Freddi crouched beside an open inspection panel. "How's it going with the new computer personality?" I asked.

"Nearly there." He glanced up. "How's our passenger?"

"Sleeping, I think. He looked awful when I showed him to his room. I don't think he likes spaceships much."

"The man doesn't like spaceships, he doesn't like space stations – what's he doing working in space?"

"He's probably traumatised after what happened. Not everyone can paint over the cracks as easy as Keya."

"I suppose." Freddi stood up from behind the workstation and wiped his hands on the seat of his trousers. "Right, the new personality is all ready to go. Do you want to be the first to talk to her, Captain?"

"Are you sure?"

He nodded. "She's waiting."

I looked up at the computer's speakers embedded in the ceiling. "Hello, Ellen?"

"Hello, Captain Cassandra." The female voice was calm, matter-of-fact and sounded more mature than I was expecting. But I liked it.

"Just call me Cassy," I said.

"Hello, Cassy," came her reply.

Freddi looked at me, nervously. "Is she okay?"

"She's perfect."

I caught a quick glimpse of his smile before he bobbed down again behind the workstation and began replacing the inspection hatch.

In the relative quiet that followed, it seemed to me that the sound of the engines had changed tone.

"Do the engines sound different to you?" I said.

Freddi picked up a screw from the small pile next to his feet and pushed it into a hole in the inspection plate with a screwdriver. "They sound like engines."

"Listen!" The pitch of their powerful rumble had shifted downward and the vibrations running through my feet didn't feel as strong.

Freddi paused with the screwdriver still in his hand. His expression changed as he heard what I heard: a steady loss of power.

"We're slowing down," he said. He let go of the screwdriver and it clattered to the floor.

"Ellen," I called up to the speakers. "What's happening with the engines?"

"Engines are functioning normally," came her calm, matter-of-fact reply.

"They sound like they're losing power," I said.

"We are slowing ahead of full stop," said Ellen.

Freddi stood up from behind the workstation. "It's still hours until we're far enough away from inhabited space to initiate q-burst."

"Ellen, check the coordinates I set when we left Leontes Station in case there are any errors."

"I apologise, Cassy, that I cannot," said Ellen. "Those coordinates were overridden while I was offline."

I glared at Freddi.

"Don't look at me," he said. "I only disabled higher functions to install the new personality. It couldn't possibly have affected our flight path."

"If I may," interjected Ellen from above. "The new coordinates were set from the control room. The control room is currently occupied by Doctor Muna Raymon."

"Raymon?" I reached across the workstation and hit the communications. "Doctor Raymon, this is the Captain – please respond." I waited for a reply, but all I heard was the slowing engines. "Doctor Raymon, this is the Captain – respond!" I took my finger off the communications control. "What the vac is he playing at?"

"We need to get up there," said Freddi, heading for the door.

"Ellen," I called out. "Restore engines to full power."

"I apologise, Cassy, that I cannot. Engine commands have been locked down from the control room."

"Drakh!" I ran after Freddi.

The ship shook as if the floor had been yanked from underneath me. I had to step sideways to regain my balance.

"Must be reverse engines kicking in," said Freddi.

"What's he trying to do?" I said. "Stop the ship or shake it to pieces?"

I was starting to feel less angry that Raymon had taken control of the ship and more worried about what he was going to do with it. I broke into a run.

Freddi's footsteps quickened behind me. But, with his bad hip, he could never run as fast as me and I reached the control room moments ahead of him.

Coming to a halt in the wide space that was built for a crew of five, I saw Raymon standing at the central console – *my* console, with its two screens. He turned to face me with two, terrified, pale blue eyes.

"Doctor Raymon, what are you doing?"

"I have to get to Fertilla," he said and broke into a fit of coughing. Spittle flew out of his mouth and dropped on the screen in front of him.

"We're already going to Fertilla!"

"You said it would be hours," he wheezed.

"Of course," I said. "We have to travel a safe distance from Leontes in normal space before we can fire up the QED."

"But I can't wait hours!"

Freddi ran through the doorway and stopped at my side. "What's he doing?" he whispered.

"Slowing down the ship to reach our destination faster," I replied.

Raymon was shaking. I could almost smell his fear as his sweat released pheromones into the air. He turned his manic stare away from us and looked back at the console.

"Step away from the controls!" I ordered. I wished I had strapped my EE weapon to my thigh, but in the safety of my own ship I hadn't thought I would need it.

"I need to initiate q-burst," said Raymon. He coughed again and spat over the screens.

"We're too close to inhabited space!" I yelled.

Raymon touched the controls. "I can't wait. I have to wormhole away."

"No!" I rushed at him, grabbed his shoulders with both hands and flung him aside.

Raymon staggered backwards, but his plump body was too heavy for me to throw far and he recovered quickly. He started back towards the console, but Freddi had manoeuvred behind him. He flung his arms around Raymon's waist and yanked him back.

As the men struggled, I swung round to view the console. Calculations flowed down the left screen in a waterfall of numbers. On the right, an animation of an opening wormhole played out in front of me.

Panicking, my fingers darted over the controls as I brought up the status of the Quantum Entanglement Drive.

Raymon continued to struggle in Freddi's grip. He was thrashing in such a crazed manner that I thought he might break free.

The computer's voice spoke from above. "Q-burst initiating."

Raymon visibly relaxed.

"Ellen, no!" I screamed, even though I knew the process couldn't be interrupted. I slammed my hand on the controls for the QED, but it was locked into operation using coordinates which could throw us out anywhere in the Obsidian Rim.

A rumble like approaching thunder gripped the ship. I grabbed the console and felt the familiar, unpleasant feeling of my guts lurching forward as the QED engaged.

Raymon pulled away from Freddi and leant forward to throw up the contents of his stomach. A stinking yellow soup of bile and half-digested food splashed onto the floor.

I fought back my own sickness as the pain of being thrust into the wormhole crushed in on my body. The G-force made it hard to breathe, but I clung on. Beside me, Freddi also held onto the nearest console.

The pain was something that had to be endured to cheat the physics of spacetime and traverse light years in the blink of an eye, but Raymon seemed to be suffering far worse than us. He screamed through a rasping throat like a terrified child. He tried to run away, but slipped in his own vomit and crashed to the floor.

He gasped for air and coughed it back out again in a series of ugly, gurgling breaths.

A flash of light seemed to bypass my eyes and burn directly into my retinas as we were pushed further into the wormhole, like falling into the deadly fire of a sun with its inescapable gravity. Then black as we switched from being pulled in, to being pushed out.

We jolted into normal space so violently I was thrown against the back wall. My spine slammed against metal as the ship lurched sideways and I slid helplessly along the panel. When I reached the gap of the doorway, I fell through it and sprawled backwards onto the corridor floor. I scrambled onto my hands and knees to get back up, but another jolt knocked me over again. It felt like the ship had rammed into something solid.

My head pounding, I crawled back into the control room. Coloured lights flickered across my eyes and I thought, for a moment, I had been knocked out and this was some after-effect of concussion. But, pulling myself to my feet, I realised the lights were not in my head – they were in my ship. Swirls of red, blue and green wound their way across the front three consoles and drifted up to the ceiling where they passed through the metal as if its existence was merely an illusion.

Freddi was at his console.

Raymon struggled for breath in the puddle of his vomit.

"What the vac is that?" I asked Freddi, looking up at the swirling coloured lights.

He didn't take his eyes off the screen. "I think it's the outer edge of the Rim."

"Are you sure?"

Travel beyond the Obsidian Rim was impossible, just like travel to the centre of the galaxy was impossible. The Oblivion War had trapped humanity in a prison of its own making between the destabilised dead zones once inhabited by our ancestors and the external barrier that marked the edge of the galaxy. No amount of qubition could ignite a q-burst strong enough to ride a wormhole through to the other side.

"It's the only explanation." Freddi stopped operating the controls and stared at the screen. "Drakh!"

"What's wrong?" I said.

"I don't know how the vac Raymon did it, but the front of the ship is embedded in the scrambled magnetic barrier."

"How is that even possible?"

"It isn't. At least, it shouldn't be."

I looked to the ceiling. "Ellen, can we use the engines to pull us out?"

"Unknown," she said. "I have no data."

I frowned. "How about q-burst?"

"Q-burst would be possible," said Ellen. "But conditions on the edge of the Rim mean that wormholes will not form."

"It's suicide," said Freddi. "Chances are, the energy will rebound right back at us and we'll be vaporised."

"Then what do you suggest?"

Freddi shrugged as Raymon took a sharp intake of breath and launched into another horrendous coughing fit.

"He's really sick," said Freddi.

"Let's worry about that when we return to normal space," I said.

But Freddi was staring at Raymon. The doctor rolled over onto his side where he managed shallow, laboured breaths.

"Freddi!" I shook him by the elbow. "Hey, Freddi! We need to get back to normal space."

"Yes, Captain." He brought his attention back to me. "The only option we have is the normal space engines."

"Then, let's try the engines. Can you fire some trial bursts? Enough to see if they have any effect, but not too much to kill us if they backfire?"

Freddi nodded. "Yeah, I can do that."

I looked at my console. The screens were full of crazy data that I didn't know how to interpret. Everything was reading as outside its normal range, and some of the sensors were fluctuating so much it was impossible to tell if the reports were real or being sent haywire by the magnetic field around us.

"Firing a one-second burst…" said Freddi. "Now!"

The sound of energy rising beneath us quickly fell again. The ship shuddered, but I remained on my feet. The screens danced with data and then settled.

"Did we move?" I said.

"Not sure. Trying again."

A brief, faint rumble beneath us; a slight shudder; a dance of data.

The ribbons of light continued to swirl at the front of the control room, but there seemed fewer of them.

"Keep going," I encouraged Freddi.

Tiny blast after tiny blast, we edged away from the barrier. The lights swirled out through the hull of the ship so there were fewer and fewer of them until they disappeared altogether. My screens settled down to a series of readings close to normal.

We were free.

"Freddi, you're amazing!"

"I only did what you told me."

But our celebration was short lived as Raymon's wheezy breaths turned into desperate, uncontrollable coughing.

"Oh my Deity," I said and went to help him.

Freddi put out his arm to stop me. "Cassy, don't! I've seen this sort of coughing before."

I didn't understand until I saw the terror on his face as he stared at the sick man gasping his last in front of us.

"It's the plague," said Freddi.

Raymon lifted a begging hand towards us. "Hel–" But he hadn't the breath to finish.

We watched helplessly as Raymon went into shock. His body convulsed so violently that his limbs slapped at the floor. He fought for breath like a man dying in the vacuum. Until the fight was gone and his body went limp. He lay still for a moment, sucked in a final, rasping mouthful of air and then the life went out of his eyes. He stared, unseeing, at the ceiling. His body, simply, stopped.

My boots had trodden in his vomit which had run from its initial splash zone to other parts of the control room. I had used the console where his spittle had landed. I had touched him when I pushed him away and Freddi had grabbed him with both arms. We looked at each other and realised, with horror, that we had both been contaminated.

## Chapter Four

**W**E STOOD IN Airlock A and took off our clothes. I kicked each garment over to the outer hatch and stood naked before Freddi. I shivered. Not because I was embarrassed in front of my male shipmate. Not because I was cold. But because I was scared. The plague had decimated my planet when I was a child. In a way, I was one of the lucky ones in that I was too young to have watched a loved one die that horrible death, but I had grown up with the stories and slept with the nightmares. Nightmares that came true in front of me as the illness had filled Doctor Raymon's lungs with infected mucus until he drowned surrounded by breathable air.

Freddi kicked the last of his clothes over to the hatch. He wasn't shaking, but his nervousness showed in the pale colour of his skin. It was like his blood was retreating to the core of his body to sequester itself as far away as possible from his contaminated exterior.

Freddi picked up the spray canister of disinfectant we had prepared earlier and detached the spray hose from the clip on the side.

"We probably won't get sick," I said. "We both lived through the plague on Fertilla. We have a natural immunity."

"Of course we do," he said, without any sense of conviction. "This is just a precaution."

He turned on the spray and a jet of disinfectant hit me in the stomach. I gasped as cold liquid blasted at my tummy and ran down my legs. I rubbed the stuff all over me like soap in the shower. Under my armpits, in my hair, between my legs and into my intimate parts. It got in my ears, up my nose and stung my eyes. By the time he had finished, the bitter taste of the disinfectant was in my mouth, and no matter how many times I swallowed, it wouldn't go away.

Then it was my turn to decontaminate Freddi. He showed no emotion as he turned around in front of the jet and the liquid ran down his body in little streams caused by the threads of his greying body hair and the deep scar on his back.

When we were done, we climbed into the pre-sprayed spacesuits we had waiting for us and went back to the control room to collect Raymon's body. With me gripping onto his wrists and Freddi holding onto his ankles, we struggled with him down the corridors to the airlock. Inside, beyond the lip of the inner hatch, our clothes floated in the shallow pool of liquid left from our decontamination showers.

Freddi must have seen my concerned expression through the helmet of my spacesuit. "I don't think it's a good idea to go wading back in there," he said over the communicator. "We'll tread even more of it into the corridor."

"Agreed," I said.

"We're going to have to throw him in."

The weight of his corpse was pulling at my arms and I could barely keep holding him, let alone throw him. But it was the best solution.

"Shouldn't we say some words first?" I said. "Commend him to the Deity or something?"

"If you like," said Freddi.

I looked down at the man's corpse. I had forgotten to close his eyes and his cold, deathly stare looked straight through me. I shivered. We had no time for words. Those who needed to mourn him could do so in their own time and in their own way.

"We throw after three," I said over the communicator. "One. Two. Three."

We swung him as best we could and he splashed down about a metre from our feet in the centre of the airlock. Freddi hit the controls, the inner hatch came down and sealed shut. We turned our backs on him and went to decontaminate the ship.

There was around an hour of air left in our spacesuits before we needed to resupply, which was something I wanted to avoid doing if at all possible. We spent that hour frantically cleaning everywhere Raymon had been, especially his room and the control room, until we had used up all of our disinfectant.

I met Freddi in the shuttle bay with less than five minutes of air remaining. He was carrying Raymon's bag. "It needs to be jettisoned into space," he said.

I nodded.

He threw it to the side and we both approached the shuttle. It was the only place we could be sure Raymon hadn't been.

The ramp descended and we climbed out of our spacesuits.

Both naked again, we stepped inside and sealed ourselves in. With the flesh of my thighs sticking to the co-pilot's seat, I opened the shuttle bay doors to the vacuum of space and watched on the screen as air rushed to escape through the crack, followed by our abandoned spacesuits. Raymon's bag tumbled towards the doors, got stuck in the narrow opening for a moment before the jaws widened and it was liberated into space.

I assisted Freddi to manoeuvre the shuttle outside and stop it a short distance from the ship. I reached for the communicator. "Ellen, we're ready," I told the ship's computer. "Open Airlock A."

"Yes, Cassy."

From our vantage point in the shuttle, I watched as a small hatch in the side of the ship slid open and exposed the contents to space. Liquid disinfectant sprayed out and instantly froze into ice crystals which twinkled against the backdrop of a distant sun. Raymon's frozen corpse shot out of the hatch head first like a torpedo and became entangled in the twisting debris of our clothes. Inside the ship, Ellen would be sucking out the air and turning up the heat to destroy every remaining bit of bacteria we had been unable to clean away.

Until that was complete, Freddi and I would have to wait it out in the shuttle.

I turned off the monitor and went into the back where I found a couple of blankets. I wrapped one around myself and secured it by tucking the end between my breasts like a towel and brought the other one back for Freddi. As I handed it to him, it seemed to me that he looked paler than when we had first stripped in the airlock. Without saying anything, he unfolded the blanket and draped it across his shoulders.

"Are you okay?" I asked. When clearly he was not.

"It gets harder to remember her before she got sick," he said. His eyes were moist with unshed tears as he looked, not at me, but *through* me, as if he were staring back into the past.

"This must bring back horrible memories," I said.

Ellen – his Ellen – had died in the plague. He had nursed her in her final days, he once told me, but all he could do was ease her passing.

"I don't want to talk about it," he said. He turned away and started playing with the shuttle controls, even though there was nothing to be done but sit there and wait.

"We need to go back to Leontes and warn them," I said.

"I'm sure they know already."

I shot him a questioning look. "You think Raymon infected the station?"

"I think the plague was confined to Fertilla where it burned itself out years ago," said Freddi. "I think that Leontes is a science research station. I think if the plague has suddenly turned up on Leontes that the two things are not unconnected."

I felt suddenly hot and loosened my blanket. "Then we stay away."

"No, we have to go back," said Freddi. "Raymon was in such a panic when he engaged the QED, that I have no idea where we are. The easiest way to get back is to follow the wormhole data that brought us here. Leontes has medical facilities which we can use, so it makes sense to stop there before heading back to Fertilla."

"Assuming they're not all dead from the plague."

"Yeah," said Freddi. "Assuming that."

# Chapter Five

The way Keya came aboard my ship made me more scared than even watching Raymon die on the control room floor. She wore a full biohazard suit that covered her entire body in impermeable yellow evi-plastic. Only a clear window of evi-plastic in the suit's hood allowed her to see out and me to see in to her concerned eyes. Through the translucent barrier between us, I noted she still wore her make-up, but her smile was gone.

She brought with her a trolley of scientific instruments she planned to use to study us. She began by asking me and Freddi to roll up our sleeves so she could take a blood sample for analysis. After everything we had been through, the pinprick from the needle offered no pain.

She fed our blood into one of her machines and we waited.

The temperature in the crew lounge was ambient, but I was hot and, where my blanket finished, my sweat made the skin of my legs stick to the padded couch. I looked across at Freddi sitting next to me, but he avoided my gaze. I think he was scared, too, but trying to hide it from me. Neither of us had developed any symptoms of the plague on the way back to Leontes Station, other than those that could be put down to anxiety, but it didn't mean we were in the clear.

"So no one else got sick on Leontes?" I asked.

Keya's voice came through a microphone clipped to her collar inside the suit and relayed through a tiny speaker on her chest. It made her sound distant, almost robotic. "No," she said.

"Perhaps it wasn't infectious," I said.

"If it was the plague, like you described, it would have been very infectious," she said.

"Then perhaps that's not what it was," I said.

Freddi pointed accusingly at Keya. "Do you think she would come in here dressed like that if it wasn't?"

"I'm only taking sensible precautions," said Keya.

Freddi dismissed her. "I lived through the plague on Fertilla, remember? I know what the man died of."

"Are you sure, Freddi?" I said. "It was a long time ago."

I put a comforting hand on his arm, but he pulled it away. "I nursed Ellen for six days – *six days* – while she coughed her lungs out and struggled for breath, in pain and in fear, before she died. That memory will live with me forever."

"Doctor Raymon died within a day," I said. "He might have been ill when we met on Leontes Station, but he wasn't that sick."

"I'm telling you, it was the plague," said Freddi. "Possibly a faster acting, genetically engineered version of the plague. Not that I need to tell Keya, because she already knows. Don't you, Keya?"

"I don't know what you mean," she said.

She had her head turned sideways to me so I couldn't see her face through the evi-plastic.

"What are you researching on this station, exactly?" said Freddi.

She didn't reply.

I looked straight at her. After what we'd been through, I wanted an answer. "Keya?"

She faced us so we could both see her clearly through the window of her suit. "One of the teams here had been working on the Fertillan plague until recently," she admitted.

"Of course they were," said Freddi. "Doctor Raymon was on that team, I'm assuming."

"He was," admitted Keya. "He realised he had become infected and left instructions for decontamination. Foolish, really, because we could have helped him."

"So he came onto my ship and tried to infect us?" I said.

"It seems he wasn't thinking clearly," said Keya. "I think the infection affected his higher functions. His message was garbled, to say the least. From what I understand, he was trying to get back to see his family. Again, foolish, because he only would have infected them."

Keya's machine pinged. It was a delicate, bright sound which seemed ironic considering the potentially ominous nature of its results.

Keya turned to the machine. I think I actually stopped breathing as I waited for her to read what it said. "You're clear," she said. "You're not going to die of the plague."

I let out a lungful of anxious air. I didn't realise how worried I had been until I heard those words. My body, which had become increasingly tense since I had sat waiting it out in the shuttle with

Freddi, suddenly relaxed and I collapsed back into the couch.

Freddi actually fell sideways and had to put out a hand to steady himself.

"But the results confirm you were exposed," said Keya. "Both of you have a very healthy collection of antibodies running around your systems. It suggests a natural immunity, probably dating from the original outbreak on Fertilla."

She reached up to the hood of her suit and unzipped it. She prised back the evi-plastic from around her face and breathed the air of my spaceship.

"Why would anyone take the risk of playing around with the Fertillan plague?" I asked Keya.

"We can learn a lot from studying it."

"You're not making a biological weapon?" I said.

"No! We were trying to make a vaccine."

I searched her face, no longer hiding behind a translucent membrane, and believed what she was saying.

"Why would you need a vaccine?" said Freddi. "Surely the plague died out."

"As far as we know," she said.

I shivered. The thought of thousands of people on a planet dying the same horrific death as Doctor Raymon was truly terrifying.

"So, what are you going to do now?" asked Keya.

"Continue with the job we were hired to do," I said. "Deliver the fertiliser then find another freelance job."

"It needs to be a lucrative one," said Freddi. "We burned through two lots of qubition going to wherever we went and back again, thanks to the mad infected doctor. A small job like a cargo run won't earn us enough."

"Maybe it's time to take your prince up on his offer," said Keya. "Let him hire you and make sure he pays the top rate."

# Chapter Six

THE FERTILLAN GUARD uniform was scratchy and went right up to my neck where it tightened around my throat like it was about to strangle me.

"Stop fidgeting!" Stephen said, as I squirmed inside the material.

We were in his bedchamber and he had decided that disguising myself as a member of the Fertillan Guard was a good idea. I disagreed.

"This is never going to work, Stephen," I said, unbuttoning the top button so I could breathe again.

"It's the only way to find out what James is up to, I told you." He reached up to the two sides of my collar and pulled them back to their strangulation-tight position.

I put my hands over his before he could secure the button. "You're in charge of the Fertillan Guard. If you want one of the people on his ship to spy on Prince James, you could ask them."

He did not release his hands, but stepped closer to me so our foreheads were nearly touching. Close enough for me to smell the soap he used to wash with, mixed with his own, alluring masculine scent. "The personnel assigned to my brother are more loyal to him than they are to me, I cannot trust them."

"He's never going to accept me as a Fertillan–"

Stephen's face moved closer still and silenced me with a kiss. The taste of him was tempting, but I overcame my desire and pulled back. His fingers slipped from my collar and his hands fell away.

"When you said you would hire me, I thought you would hire me and my ship," I said.

"You told me Freddi was taking your ship to be checked for damage after your encounter with the edge of the Rim."

"That's not the point!" I was angry now. He had lured me into working for him because of the money and because it would give us more of a chance to see each other, but I was beginning to think I was right in the first place – bed and business don't mix.

Stephen began to chuckle. It only made me angrier.

"What?" I said.

He looked me up and down. "I never thought it was possible for someone to look sexy in that uniform."

"I don't look sexy. I feel ridiculous."

The brown trousers and jacket were cut with straight, unflattering lines in a thick material that lent itself to standing to attention, not softening with my body as I moved. Like any uniform, it turned me into a non-person. An automaton to conform alongside all the other automatons and be ordered about without question.

"Cassy, you would look sexy in a sack."

I could see he was making a compliment and so I decided to take it at face value and calm myself down. "I still don't think it's a good plan."

"You could try to follow him in your ship," said Stephen, "but if it enters a wormhole, you'll only have minutes to replicate his calculations to ascertain his destination before he disappears. Even if you manage to get that information, knowing he's travelled to Serilla or Raeaa or Sendat isn't going to help me find out why. Anyway, to follow his ship you would need to be close enough for him to see your ship and you would be discovered."

"Whereas he won't see me at all when I'm standing right next to him inside his ship!" I said, sarcastically.

Stephen sighed. "He won't know who you are. You've walked past him maybe once in Londos House. And no one is going to recognise you in that uniform."

"It'll be obvious I'm not a Fertillan Guard. I'll stick out like a sore thumb."

"Stand up straight when a superior officer is talking to you, do what you're told and throw in a 'yes sire' or two and you'll be fine. I'll give you a few lessons if you like."

I fidgeted again. "I don't know…"

"Look…" He came forward again, pulled together the two halves of my collar and secured the button. He brushed back the hair from my face and I savoured the touch of his fingers across my scalp. "We need to do something with your hair."

I shook my hair to free it from him, then gathered up the long, dark strands myself and pulled them back into a ponytail. "Have you got an elastic band or something?"

Stephen rubbed his hand across his own short, brown hair.

"Not something I have call for."

I plaited my hair into a braid and wound it round itself into a makeshift bun which I had to hold in place at the top of my head. "What about that?"

He nodded. "Very… military."

He turned round and reached for the chair where I had dumped my own, much more comfortable clothes and rifled through them. Buried underneath, he found the peaked hat that belonged to the uniform and brought it over.

He placed the hat over the bun. I slipped out my hand and my hair stayed encased inside. Then he came round to the front and pulled the peak down so I could see it at the top of my field of vision. "There we go."

"I must look stupid," I said.

"No, you don't." He took my hand and led me across his bedchamber to where a wardrobe, three times the size of my own back on the ship, stood along the side wall. He threw open the doors and revealed two rails full of clothes, all in fine fabric, except for three copies of his own Fertillan Guard uniform squashed up one end. One of the doors had a full-length mirror inside. He took my shoulders and turned me round to face it.

I saw the full horror of my own reflection. The uniform covered every part of me apart from my hands and a small part of my face from my eyes to my chin. It was drab, bland, brown and unflattering.

"Stand up straight!" Stephen barked in my ear, like it was an order.

I snapped to sort-of attention and my image in the mirror became more soldier-like.

Only a few stray strands of hair, which had escaped my impromptu bun, hung down at my neck and gave me away.

"See?" said Stephen.

I turned round to face him and away from my hideous reflection. "If Prince James has a detail of his own Fertillan Guard assigned to him, won't he realise I'm not one of them?"

"You'll be replacing one of his regulars who will be called away on other duties. It will all appear routine."

"I'm still not sure, Stephen. I'm not a spy."

"Just hang around his spaceship and report back what you see. I'm not expecting you to plant bugging devices or hack into his personal files. And if, for any reason, you're found out, then you say you are working for me. But I am your trump card, Cassy. I would be grateful if you didn't reveal our connection unless absolutely necessary. James will tell King Richard and that would be… awkward."

"Your other brother," I reminded myself.

"He doesn't like me very much as it is. You know how brothers are."

"Not really. I don't have any brothers or sisters."

"Then you are lucky. My relationship with Richard is as fractious as my relationship with James. Except, being the King, he has more power."

"So," I said, feeling that I was going regret my words as soon as I said them. "When and where do you need me for this spying mission of yours?"

He grinned. "You shall receive your orders in due course, Guardswoman Cassandra."

"Good. Now, can I take off this vacking uniform?"

I undid the top button and felt the blissful release at my throat.

"Let me help you with that," said Stephen. He undid the second button.

I loved it when he undressed me.

With a surge of excitement, we both fumbled with buttons until I was free of the jacket. I threw it over in the vague vicinity of the chair and Stephen propelled me backwards towards the bed as I pulled off the undershirt and he grabbed at the belt around my trousers.

"I know I said you look good in that uniform," he whispered in my ear. "But you look even better out of it."

I giggled as he finished undressing me and we threw ourselves onto the neatly made bed where our sex unruffled the covers and left the sheets damp with sweat.

Twice.

# Chapter Seven

PRINCE JAMES'S SHIP was a personal transport and small compared to my ship and most other QED-enabled vessels I had been on. It had no cargo hold, just a crew lounge with a galley and a washroom attached, private quarters for the prince, and the main flight deck.

I joined the other four Fertillan Guards – three men and a woman – on the flight deck where we stood at ease to wait for Prince James to board. This involved standing looking straight ahead with my feet apart and my hands behind my back, giving the stance all the formality of standing to attention with only part of the discomfort.

I rubbed my finger around the collar of my Fertillan Guard uniform to let in some air around my neck. How Stephen wore his stiff jacket without complaint while he was on duty, I couldn't understand. Returning my hand to the small of my back, I resumed the full 'at ease' pose which he had taught me.

"Are you okay?" whispered the female guard standing beside me.

I turned to look at her and, between the top of her buttoned-up collar and peak of her hat that shaded her forehead, I saw the light reflected in her eyes and she suddenly became a real person to me. "It's a new uniform," I explained in a half-lie. "I think they got my size wrong."

"I know what you mean," she said. "They're so stiff when you first wear them, but I think they stretch after you've worn them for a bit. Either that or you get used to it."

I didn't think I would ever get used to it.

The woman tensed at the sound of a boot on metal just outside the flight deck and she turned abruptly away from me, snapping her feet together and bringing her arms stiffly by her sides to stand to attention. I rapidly followed suit as another footstep brought Prince James into our presence.

I had seen James before, at a distance, and remembered how he resembled Stephen with the same wide Regellan family nose, blue eyes and brown hair which he grew longer than Stephen's military style. Close up, his extra weight was more apparent in the thickness of his neck and he seemed to generally take up more room than his younger brother. Which might have had something to do with the loose clothes he chose to wear: a plain white shirt embroidered with gold thread in a swirling pattern down each side of the buttons and a black jacket which smoothed the line over the slight bulge of his belly, with pads which made his shoulders appear broader. The protocol of standing to attention wouldn't let me look down at his shoes, but I knew the reason he appeared taller than Stephen was because he wore heels a little higher than most men.

"Morning," said James. The word was a friendly greeting, but his tone suggested it was merely perfunctory. "Let's get–"

He stopped when he saw me. I held myself to attention while, inside, I could feel my heart pump with adrenaline.

"Who are you?" James demanded. He looked straight into my face, invading my personal space so I could smell the coffee he had drunk for breakfast.

I kept my eyes focussed on the left ear of the male Fertillan Guard opposite to keep my face impassive. "Forestri, Sire." It was the name Stephen had given me when he had faked my credentials.

James looked around at the others as if taking a mental roll call, then stared back at me. "Where's Zelenski?"

"Temporary assignment, Sire," I said.

"Temporary assignment to what?"

"I wasn't told, Sire. I was just told to report to you, Sire." I hoped I hadn't over-done the 'sire' bit.

Fortunately, James didn't seem to notice and shrugged it off as he went over to his command chair. "Let's get out to where we can fire up the QED. I don't want to be late."

"Yes, Sire!" chorused the others. For a moment, I thought I should have joined in, but I realised that even if Forestri was a real Fertillan Guard, she would have been new to the team and being left out of certain things was going to be fine.

Prince James took up position in the central command chair while the other four went to their stations, which were built into the three forward walls of the flight deck. It left one remaining station free which I assumed was for me. I sat myself down in front of it as if I had known it was mine all along and familiarised myself with the controls. If there's one thing I *do* have expertise in, it's spaceships, and the console seemed little different to any other I had used. It had access to all the data of the ship's systems, although its designated role was to control the regular engines. That meant it was my responsibility to get us far enough away from Fertilla in normal space to engage the QED.

"Know what you're doing, Forestri?" asked Prince James from his command chair.

"Absolutely, Sire," I said, relieved I was being asked to do something so simple, and laid in a course similar to one I had used on my own ship many times.

The engines fired smoothly, we eased away from the gravitational pull of Fertilla and headed out of the system.

ONCE THE SHIP was on course for uninhabited space, the computer was left to control the basic systems while one of the guardsmen – not me, thankfully – was left to monitor things on the flight deck. I was dismissed to the crew lounge along with the other three guardsmen.

I was the first to make it into the washroom where I could finally relax. I locked the door and leant back against it with a sigh which I kept quiet enough so as not to be heard. Resting my head against the door, I found it pushed against the rim of my hat and lifted it up. The relief of not having it pressing down on my head so the relatively fresh air of the spaceship was able to drift across my hair was bliss. A couple of the others had taken their hats off once they commenced their duties, but I had kept the brim of mine pulled as far down over my eyes as I could get away with.

I reached down to the gun holster at my thigh where the Fertillan Guard-issued personal EE weapon was clipped securely. It gave me some comfort to know it was there ready to use in case I got into trouble. Of course, all the other guards and Prince James also had EEWs so I had to hope that, if it came to it, I wouldn't have to face them all in a gun fight.

The washroom was a welcome retreat, but I couldn't stay in there forever. So I used the toilet, made sure my hat was straight in the mirror and reluctantly left.

A guardsman queuing outside acknowledged me as I passed. I responded with a quick half smile and averted my eyes.

I needed to interact as little as possible with the rest of the crew. Which wasn't easy in the crew lounge which was a cramped room consisting of a couple of tiny tables, five upright chairs and what the others called a galley – a grand name for something which was barely even a kitchenette. I poured myself a cup of water – the only thing available – from a dispensing machine and took it to the chair the furthest away in the corner. The woman guard, who was sitting two chairs down, saw me alone and came to join me.

"Hello," she said with a smile. She took off her hat, revealing short black hair beneath, laid her hat on the table and gave her head a good scratch. "My head gets so hot in the vacking thing! Who ever thought wearing a hat in a warm spaceship was a good idea?"

"Yes." I didn't know what else to say. I glanced to see where the two guardsmen were. The one who had smiled at me had just come out of the washroom and had struck up a conversation with the other one by the water dispenser. Which meant they weren't going to join us any time soon. Which meant it was going to be more difficult to make my excuses and leave. Slipping away from a group of three or four people would be far less noticeable than slipping away from a group of two. Not as if there was really anywhere else to go.

"I don't think I've seen you before," said the guardswoman.

"I've been stationed on Prince Stephen's ship." Another half-lie. I had been on his ship a couple of times, but only as a passenger.

"Ooh, what's he like?" Her eyes brightened with curiosity.

"He's…" My brain finished the sentence with 'sexy, gentle, surprising and infuriating', but my mouth opted for something which wouldn't give me away. "He's okay."

"Yeah, Prince James is okay too. Being in his personal detail, I get to travel. It's better than guarding Londos House all the time."

"Yes," I said again.

"My name's Louissi." She held out her hand to shake and I accepted in what was, paradoxically, both a formal and friendly gesture.

"Isabette," I said. Isabette had been my mother's name and Stephen agreed it could be part of my undercover identity.

"Do you know where we're going?" I asked Louissi.

"Manupia," she said. "*Again!*"

"The factory planet?"

"That's the one," said Louissi. "I love the chance to get off Fertilla, but the same old journey's getting a bit boring."

"So why is Prince James going to Manupia?"

"I thought at first it had something to do with President Udinov's two daughters – they're very pretty. But it seems not. It's just business, as far as I can work out. Something to do with Manupia struggling to compete with rival manufacturers."

"What rival manufacturers?" I said. "Manupia is the factory planet. I mean, it's *The* Factory Planet."

"Not any more, they're being undercut by competitors, from what I overheard."

"What's that got to do with Prince James?"

Louissi shrugged. "Beats me. But whatever it is, it must be ever so complicated, because they keep meeting up to talk about it."

I thought about what other questions I could ask to pump her for information, but I suspected she didn't know any more than she had already told me. Besides, I needed to make sure I didn't come across as being overcurious and raise her suspicions.

"So, what do we do now? It must take more than a day to travel to and from the wormhole points in normal space." I looked around, knowing the only accommodation in the ship was the flight deck, James's office and the lounge in which we were sitting. "I mean, where do we sleep? Are we allowed to sleep?"

She laughed. It was a joyful little girl's laugh that didn't at all fit with the formal uniform she wore. "We sleep here."

I looked around, there were still only the two tables and the five chairs. "On the floor?"

"No! I don't know what sort of luxury you're used to on Prince Stephen's ship, but here we have cupboards that fold out into bunk beds."

I hadn't noticed any cupboards until I looked again and saw the recessed handles in the walls and rectangle cracks around them that indicated the outline of bed-sized panels. "Clever."

"You're lucky Zelenski isn't here. She has to be the worst snorer I've ever bunked with," said Louissi. "You don't snore, do you?"

"No," I said. "I don't think so."

"Good, because I've forgotten my earplugs." She broke into peels of high-pitched giggles in a most un-military-like manner which made me smile.

Perhaps my method to avoid detection on the small ship was not to try to be alone, but to join in. As long as I didn't give too much of my real self away.

We travelled through a wormhole with all the organisation and military precision one would expect from a crew of Fertillan Guard. Afterwards, we were allowed to sleep during most of the journey through normal space to Manupia. Well, the others slept. I mostly lay awake listening to their heavy breathing until I eventually dozed off and was woken by the shift change of the men swapping over to keep watch on the flight deck. I was still tired when the lights were turned on and the whole crew were summoned to our stations to oversee the landing procedure.

The ship was small enough to land directly on the planet's surface rather than having to take a shuttle. Communications chatter, handled by Louissi but heard by all of us, said that a car would be sent to bring Prince James to the planetary headquarters. For a moment, I was worried the prince was going to order me to stay behind – and I would lose my chance to gather more intelligence – but instead, he elected two of the men to guard the ship while myself, Louissi and the guardsman from outside the washroom, were ordered to travel with him.

The 'car' was nothing like Prince Stephen's official Fertillan car that I had once travelled in. It was more like a personnel carrier with space for six people to sit facing each other along two benches in the rear, while there were two more comfortable seats up front for a driver and a passenger. It was also airtight, as Manupia had no breathable atmosphere and the headquarters lay several miles from the landing site across open ground.

I took my seat in the back next to Louissi and opposite the smiling guardsman. Also opposite me was one local Manupian who didn't smile, but looked down at his lap where he twirled his thumbs around each other in a pointless, unending pattern. He wore a simple black uniform of trousers and shirt with an unbuttoned jacket over the top. A second Manupian sat up front in the driver's seat next to Prince James. It meant both of them got the benefit of a clear view of where we were going out of the only window at the front of the vehicle, while we could only see between their heads if we looked sideways.

As we set off, I caught a glimpse of the planet's surface and reflected on how it reminded me of Fertilla, with its dusty, yellow surface and occasional boulder sticking out of the ground. The Manupian sun was low in the sky, but still bounced off the hard, flat earth to bathe the view in a gentle, yellow light. There was no road, so it was a bumpy ride which was uncomfortable, but not unbearable. Although, if I had to endure much more than half an hour of it, I felt sure I would be ill.

A large bump knocked the vehicle sideways. I clung onto the armrests of my seat to stop me falling off it.

"What was that?" said Prince James.

"Must have been an unexpectedly large rock," said the driver.

I put my hand up to my own mask and the others did the same as we anticipated what was about to happen.

He pulled down the handle of the control. The doors clunked open a crack. Air hissed and I felt the atmosphere rush past me as it escaped out onto the planet and the icy cold rushed in. I opened my mouth to breathe, but there was no oxygen. I gasped at nothing and panicked as I realised I hadn't turned my breather on. I desperately fiddled with the controls until the canister released some of its precious contents into my mask and I sucked the air deep into my lungs.

Something flashed past the gap between the doors. A person? The gap grew wider and the Manupians opened fire. Bright white light flooded my vision while the blasts – barely an arm's length away – sounded distant in the atmosphere barely thick enough to transmit the sound waves.

The Manupians jumped out onto the planet's surface, firing as they went.

Louissi and other Fertillan Guard took up protective positions – weapons ready – in front of James.

I moved to the open doors to stand guard as the first line of defence.

Stepping forward, I saw that the Manupians' weapons fire had struck two men whose bloodied bodies lay on the dusty ground. One was clearly dead from a gaping wound in his chest, but the other was still alive. A blast had severed his arm at the elbow and a second had taken a chunk out of his side. His surviving hand and legs were floundering helpless like a baby too immature to crawl away. The man would be dead soon, either from the blood loss or shock.

I aimed my weapon at his head and summoned the courage to end his suffering.

My finger squeezed the trigger as something grabbed hold of my arm. The blast fired uselessly up into the sky and I was pulled from the transport to land hard on my back in the dust. The dark figure of my attacker stood over me and raised something which glinted in the Manupian sunlight. As it came down to crush my skull, I rolled sideways and felt the thump of the metal bar striking the ground where I had lain. I scrambled to my feet as the woman who had attacked me pivoted round and raised her weapon for a second strike. Hatred stared out of her eyes over the top of a breather mask which was attached by a line to a canister, far larger than my own, on her back.

She ran towards me with the bar lifted high. But I side-stepped and parried, turning back to her with my EEW raised. She came in for another attack, but stopped as she saw my gun.

"Drop it!" My words hardly travelled in the thin air, but I indicated with a nod what she should do and my message was clear. She lowered her arms and let the weapon go limp in her hands. It fell to her feet with a silent puff of dust.

I stole a quick glance behind me and saw no sign of fighting. There was only one of the Manupians who had sat in the back with us, walking towards me with his EE rifle held casually at his side.

I held the woman at gunpoint and waited for him to arrive. He could take her into custody and question her if he wanted. Whatever the reason for the attack, it wasn't my fight and I had no need to take responsibility for her.

As he closed in on her, I thought he was going to grab her arms and secure them behind her back, but at the last minute he grabbed at her mask and yanked it from her face. Her expression of defeat turned to terror as her means of life was snatched away. She reached out for it – her mouth opening and closing in silent pleas – as he grabbed the air line with both hands and snapped it in half. The woman fumbled for the end of the line which was still attached to the canister and pulled it towards her mouth, but the end was too short to reach. Her eyes widened in panic.

The Manupian stood with the woman's useless face mask still in his hand, watching her as she sank to her knees and clawed desperately at the buckle of the harness that held the canister on her back. Horrified, I stepped forward to help her, but the Manupian put out his arm to stop me. So I stood by as her clumsy, panicked fingers managed to free the harness, and the canister hit the ground. Gasping repeatedly for oxygen that wasn't there, she pulled at the snapped line and brought it to her lips. But, as she sucked desperately, I knew there would be no life-saving air. The valve that released the air from the canister was part of the face mask that the Manupian had ripped from her. She must have known that too, but still she sucked again and again – her skin paling with lack of oxygen – until she could suck no more.

She collapsed to the ground, unconscious. The line flopped out of her open mouth and landed in the dust.

The Manupian turned away from her and left her to die.

I felt sick that I had stood there and allowed it to happen. I should have urged her to run, at least she would have had a chance.

She probably would have ignored me.

I didn't know why she had been crazy enough to attack a transport of armed personnel with only a metal bar. But regardless of her suicidal attack, no one deserved to die like that.

I followed the Manupian around to the front of the vehicle, stepping around the body of another attacker face down in the dirt, to see what we had crashed into. It was another vehicle, but much smaller and in a much rougher condition than ours. It appeared it had deliberately been driven into our path as part of an ambush.

I stood and shivered in the cold of Manupia as the others made sure our car had suffered no serious damage. Then, with my air running low, I returned to join the others.

It took only minutes to pull the spear out of the car and repair the hole in the side panel so we could seal ourselves inside and re-pressurise the vehicle. I pulled the breather mask from my face and took the canister off my back, thankful that I didn't have to find out if there were any spares after my one had been exhausted.

# Chapter Eight

J AMES IGNORED THE protests of his guards, who insisted they should go on ahead for his own protection, and strode out of the car in a rage. He brushed aside the Manupian official who had come to greet him and marched down the wide, opulent hallway of the planet's headquarters while Louissi, the guardsman and myself hurried after him with our weapons drawn. It seemed unlikely that this was the standard protocol for arriving at the powerhouse of a fellow planetary ruler, but considering the welcome we'd had on the planet's surface, the other two clearly decided it was necessary. I merely followed their lead and tried to make it look like I knew what I was doing.

"Where's Udinov?" James shouted. "Get me Udinov now!"

He paused at an intersection and looked left and right and left again before the official he had earlier brushed aside was able to catch up and, with a breathless suggestion that he should lead the way, squeezed passed the indignant prince to take the left turn.

We continued to march, like a Fertillan invasion down the second passageway which ended with a set of impressive floor-to-ceiling double doors. The official slowed and put his ear close to the panelling as he gave it a gentle *rappity-tap-tap* knock. But he was given no time to wait for an answer, as Prince James grabbed and turned both handles, flinging the doors wide open and revealing a spacious office with a large, commanding desk at one end with an array of screens and a startled-looking man sitting behind it.

"Udinov, why the vac was I attacked?" said James, barely breaking stride as he marched into the room.

"Ah, Your Highness," said the man – who was evidently Udinov – getting to his feet and re-establishing his own decorum. "I'm afraid it was the workless."

"Attacking *me*?"

"Their attacks are getting more brazen. I apologise, but this is the first time any violence has been reported outside of the cities."

"You need to keep a handle on this, Udinov, we're not ready to proceed."

"Yes, we have a lot to discuss," said Udinov with remarkable smoothness. "Let me fetch you some refreshments and we can get down to business."

James approached the open doorway, glowered at the three of us and the hapless official, then firmly pushed both doors shut in our faces. The latch secured itself with a subtle, but definitive *click*.

The official quietly slunk away while Louissi about-turned with a military step and stood to attention to the left of the double doors. I did the same and stood on the right. The guardsman marched to the end of the corridor where he stopped and took up position to watch from there.

I tried listening to what was going on behind the doors, but the material was thick and I couldn't hear anything. After many long minutes in which I thought I might topple over or faint – or both – Louissi changed her stance to being at ease. I followed suit and we stood there like that, looking straight ahead and saying nothing for a couple of hours of extreme tedium.

THE OPENING OF the double doors pulled me out of my daze. Louissi instinctively brought herself to attention. I did the same and felt the blood stir into pins and needles in my left foot.

James and Udinov walked out in more jovial mood than when they had entered. James had dispensed with his jacket and Udinov was resting his hands in his trouser pockets in a casual fashion.

"It's unfortunate you won't be visiting the Jonsonii factory on this occasion," said Udinov. "You could really get a sense of what we plan to do if you were there."

"After my journey here, Udinov, I think I've had enough excitement for one day," said James.

"I understand completely. That doesn't stop us having dinner, however. I've invited Helinea and Sophea to join us. It will help keep business off the dinner table."

They continued to chatter like that, all politeness and smiles, as they ambled along to wherever they were going. Louissi broke into a march to follow them and I tried to copy her example, but keeping a regular rhythm behind two men who were doing completely the opposite was near-on impossible. I was able to stay close enough to eavesdrop, but it did nothing to forward my information-gathering mission, as all they talked about was dinner, which made my stomach complain. It had been several hours since my rudimentary breakfast of crackers spread with unidentifiable tasteless brown stuff in the crew lounge and I was hungrier than I realised.

The men disappeared into another room and left Louissi and myself abandoned in the hallway again. The male Fertillan Guard joined us and suggested he swap with me so I could stretch my legs a bit more and stand to watch further down the hall.

As I walked back the way we had come, I passed two women in long swish dresses walking in the other direction. They were young enough to be Udinov's daughters – presumably the Helinea and Sophea he had referred to – and were, as per Louissi's description, very pretty. With their long, silky hair and dresses of fine-weave material that followed the subtle curves of their perfectly proportioned bodies, they made me feel very drab in my brown uniform. They took no notice of me, of course, and I felt they might have walked straight into me if I hadn't stepped aside to let them pass.

At the end of the corridor, I could have stayed on guard for another period of extreme tedium, but as I turned to go through the motions of standing to attention, I realised I was looking directly down the passageway that led to Udinov's office. The same office I had seen earlier with its array of screens. It seemed to me, it would be foolish to have gone to all that effort, to have come all that way, not to at least have a little snoop about.

I approached the doors, glanced behind to check no one was watching, and turned one of the handles so the door clicked open. It revealed the office to be almost exactly as I had glimpsed it earlier, except for two chairs pushed out from the desk from where James and Udinov must have been sitting. One of the chairs had James's jacket draped over the back. I sneaked in, closed the door as silently as I could behind me, and went over to the jacket. The material was soft to the touch and slightly heavier than I might have expected. I checked the pockets and found he had left his P-tab in there. A moment of excitement at the thought of getting into it and finding out the information he had stored in there was quelled by the realisation that I had no way of breaking through his security settings. In any case, stealing it was probably a bad idea and if Stephen had wanted to rifle through his brother's P-tab, he would have found a much better opportunity to do so at Londos House.

The bigger prize was Udinov's personal computer system. To my delight, it was still activated. I sat down and pulled up the chair nearest to the central screen.

Not as if I knew what to look for. With no information on what James was doing on Manupia, I was flying blind.

I pulled up a list of recently accessed files. At the top was something titled *Jonsonii Factory* – the same place Udinov had mentioned. I went to open the file, but the computer emitted a disgruntled tone and displayed a message asking for Udinov's passphrase.

Drakh!

Even if I knew what his passphrase was, it would probably be linked to his voice pattern and I would still be locked out.

I scrolled down the list to see if there was anything I could glean from the titles. Most of them meant nothing to me. One, however, was called *Workless*. I tried to open it and, to my surprise, the computer let me in without complaining.

At the same time I heard the door click.

I jumped to my feet. Looking around in panic, realising there was nowhere to hide, I grabbed James's jacket.

The door swung open to reveal James himself, conspicuous in his unjacketed white tailored shirt. "Forestri?"

James stared at me.

"One of the headquarters staff said you'd left your jacket here, Sire," I said. "I didn't want to disturb you, Sire, so I thought I would collect it and keep it safe for you."

"Hmm. I am perfectly capable of collecting my own jacket."

"Yes, Sire."

I didn't like the way he was looking at me. He wasn't angry, he wasn't upset. He seemed curious.

"I should get back to my duties," I walked up to him, handed him his jacket and headed for the open door, trying to make it look like I wasn't in a hurry.

"Forestri!" he ordered.

I stopped. I feared he had seen me looking at Udinov's screens. I feared he realised that a person who goes into a room simply to collect a jacket, doesn't close the door behind them.

"Turn round, Forestri, and take off your hat."

The freelancer part of me wanted to tell him to vac off. I wanted to run away and face the consequences later. But where could I run to? My only way off the planet was in Prince James's ship.

I turned. I removed my hat. The protective brim that kept part of my features hidden was gone.

"I've seen you somewhere before," he said. "I thought as much when I came on board the ship, but I dismissed it because I've seen a lot of Fertillan Guards."

"Perhaps on duty at Londos House, Your Highness," I suggested.

"I thought that was the case, which is why I dismissed it, but without your hat…"

He stepped forward and lifted his hand. I flinched, but he didn't hit me. He reached round to the back of my head where I had tied my hair into a bun and pulled out the pins that secured it. My hair fell down around my shoulders.

"Now I know where I've seen you before," he said. "You're my brother's whore!"

He grabbed me by the arm and dragged me from the room.

"I don't know what you mean!" I protested. But if he really recognised me from our only brief encounter in Londos House, then nothing I said would make a difference.

Louissi and the guardsman were waiting outside, having obviously followed him down the hall. I only caught a glimpse of the shock of their faces before I was thrown to the floor at their feet.

"Arrest her!" ordered James.

"Sire?" said Louissi.

"Take her into custody. Lock her up. Do whatever you have to do, but keep her out of my sight until we get back to Fertilla."

"Yes, Sire," said the guardsman.

"Yes, Sire," said Louissi.

# CHAPTER NINE

JAMES PULLED ME by the collar of my Fertillan Guard uniform into Londos House, half strangling me as I was forcibly taken down the corridors with my arms flailing and my feet barely touching the floor. He threw open the door of Stephen's office. It was empty: just his desk and a chair tucked neatly underneath. He yanked me round and marched through more corridors to Stephen's bedchamber. He went straight in without knocking, but Stephen's bed was made, the room smelt freshly clean and there was no sign of Stephen. James pulled me back, without turning me round, so the collar cut into my throat. I lost my footing and I was dragged, like a sack, back the way we had come with my feet trying to find purchase on the floor.

James flung open the door to the ornate sitting room where Stephen and I had once drunk tea together. Stephen sat on the plush yellow sofa with its gold embroidery, dressed in his Fertillan Guard uniform as he consulted his P-tab. He appeared to be having an informal meeting with a guardswoman who was sitting next to him.

"You! Out!" James barked at the guardswoman.

The woman jumped to her feet. She took half a step forward before realising she had left her hat on the room's polished wooden tea table. She grabbed it, secured it on her head and scuttled out.

James waited until she shut the door behind her, then threw me across the floor. "What was your whore doing on board my ship?" he demanded.

I splayed, head first, towards the table and it was all I could do to stop myself bashing into it and knocking myself out.

"James…" said Stephen, standing to face him. "There's no need to use offensive language."

"Planting someone in my security detail to spy on me is what I find offensive," said James.

I pulled myself up to sitting and shuffled along on the carpet to rest my back against the sofa.

Stephen looked down at me with concern. "Are you okay, Cassy?"

I pulled at the collar around my neck to loosen the material. I was shaken and possibly bruised, but I was not hurt. "Yeah, I'm fine."

"So, you admit you know this woman?" yelled James.

"I admit nothing," said Stephen, "until you explain why you keep leaving Fertilla to go off on some secret mission."

James scoffed. "For the Deity's sake, Stevie, it's not a secret mission. I visit other systems to broker trade deals, you know that. The only reason we live like this–" He waved his arms to indicate the opulence all around us. "–is because I secure a good price for our food exports. It's certainly more than you do, wandering around in your pretentious uniform playing soldier!"

Stephen brushed away the insult. "If it's not a secret, then tell me."

"Like you told me about your whore?"

"My personal life is my business, whereas your dealings on other worlds is the whole family's business."

"You get her pregnant and the child claims inheritance, then it affects all of us."

"That's not going to happen."

"I still want to hear about your whore, Stevie. Give me all the details: the way her breasts dance when she climbs on top of you, the way she squeals when she pleasures you."

"Hey!" I pulled myself to my feet and confronted James. With both of us standing, it reminded me how much taller and physically stronger he was than me. But I was angry and insulted. "I don't care who you are, you don't get to talk about me like that."

Stephen turned to me with a stern face and it was difficult to tell who he was annoyed at: me or his brother. "Sit down, Cassy."

"No!"

"Please."

"Having trouble keeping your whore in check, Stevie?"

Stephen stepped towards James so unexpectedly, that his brother flinched. "You should keep your mouth in check, James. You have a problem with me, you sort it out with me. Don't take it out on innocent women."

"Innocent?" James scoffed. "She was spying on me."

"What option did I have when you won't tell me what you're doing?"

James leant right into Stephen's face. "You keep your nose out of my business and I'll keep my nose out of your bedroom."

"My business is the security of the planet," said Stephen. "If you keep disappearing without saying where you're going, then that puts our security at risk."

James's composure fell away and his face reddened with anger. "What endangers Fertilla is sending an untrained whore to guard the heir to the throne while he's on another planet. I'm sure Richard will agree with me when I explain all this to him."

"You're only heir to the throne until Richard has children. From what I hear about his love life, that might not be too long."

James took in a long breath and allowed it to inflate his chest. "King Richard *will* be informed, you have my promise," he said. "Meanwhile, you need to keep *your* love life out of my business."

He turned his back on his brother and headed for the door where he stopped and looked back. But not at Stephen – at me.

"And *you*, Individual Sesaan Cassandra." He spat out my name like it was dirt. "You should watch yourself and think about what happened to your mother."

I went cold. My mother's death was no secret, it was on my file, but to use it against me like some kind of threat was cruel.

James slammed the door shut behind him and the whole room shuddered.

Stephen apologised to me a thousand times.

He took me to his bedchamber – but there was no sexual motive – he chose it because it was quiet and private.

He left me to wash in his private bathroom and I delighted in the luxury of the warm water and the ostentatious lather of soap to clean the smell of sweat from my body. When I emerged in a towel, he had my own clean clothes waiting for me and a meal consisting of a ham sandwich made with real ham from a real pig.

Still wrapped in a towel, I ate it hungrily, and drank the whole jug of water which had been provided. It was only then that the fatigue and stress of the mission, along with two nights of barely any sleep, caught up with me.

He laid me in his bed. Again, there was nothing sexual in his gesture. He pulled the covers gently over me, turned out the lights, and let me sleep.

When I woke, Stephen was sitting on the shiny wooden chair with one leg casually crossed over the other and looking at his P-tab. The light from the small screen lit up his face with a soft glow and I saw his look of concentration before the sound of me moving in the bedclothes caused him to look up.

"Morning, Cassy." He smiled.

I brushed the mess of my hair from my face, but still felt dozy. "It's morning?"

"Yeah."

I realised he had changed out of his Fertillan Guard uniform and was in a casual shirt and trousers of light grey. It had to be the next day. "How long did I sleep?"

Stephen checked his P-tab. "A little over twelve hours."

I sighed and looked across at the other side of the bed to where Stephen would normally lay. That half of the bedclothes remained tucked in and the pillow undented. "Did you sleep?"

"I took the guest room. You looked so comfortable, I didn't want to disturb you." He turned off the P-tab and put it in his pocket. "Do you want breakfast?"

"Food again?" It didn't seem long since I had last eaten.

"Is that a 'no'?" he asked.

"No!" I said, sitting up. "I mean, yes. It's a 'yes'. I'd love breakfast."

Stephen got the kitchen to rustle up some tea and toast with a spoonful of thick yogurt on the side and three tiny red berries which burst in my mouth with a rush of juice that was both sweet and sharp at the same time. Afterwards, I put on my clothes and sat on the end of the bed.

"Are you sure you're okay, Cassy?" he asked.

"I'm fine."

"They didn't mistreat you?"

"No."

"I'm sorry I asked you to go."

"Don't be," I said. "I agreed to it."

"Do you want to tell me what happened?"

I shrugged. "I got caught."

Stephen smiled. "I meant, before that."

I sighed. I wasn't entirely sure what to make of it myself. "Your brother, Prince James, has been going to Manupia."

"Manupia? The factory planet?"

"That's the one."

"What does he want there?"

I shrugged again. "Whatever it is, it appears he's been negotiating with President Udinov for some time."

"A trade deal?" suggested Stephen.

"Seems unlikely," I said. "Not for food, anyway. Fertilla must have deals to export food to hundreds of places, they can't take multiple visits and the personal attention of a president to negotiate. You know what it's like out in the Obsidian Rim. If Manupia doesn't agree to buy food at a price Fertilla is selling it for, there's plenty of other places that will."

"If not a trade deal, then what?"

"I suspect it might have something to do with the workless. They've been causing problems in Manupian cities, apparently."

"I haven't heard of that term before," said Stephen. "People who want to work less? Factory work is tough and laborious, but the people on Manupia are supposed to have a strong work ethic. They're dedicated to their factories, which is why the planet is so successful in manufacturing – or so the propaganda goes."

"I think it might mean people without a job. Like 'topless', without a top; or 'childless', without children. Manupia has been having some trouble with competition, from what I heard, which probably has something to do with it."

"That doesn't explain what that might have to do with James."

"No, it doesn't," I said. "But Udinov was very keen for him to tour one of the factories. I didn't discover why, but I could go back and find out."

"Cassy, no," Stephen said. "You've done enough."

"But now we have more to go on. We know where he's been going and we think it has something to do with the factories. What's the point in having leads if we don't follow up on them?"

"What are you suggesting? You can't go back on James's ship."

"I'm a freelance spaceship captain, I can go anywhere. Manupia doesn't use freelancers much, but there is a little bit of work there. I can use that pretence to go back to the planet and have a snoop around."

"No, Cassy. At least with the Fertillan Guard you were somewhat under my protection, but go on your own and you'll *be* on your own."

"I have Freddi."

He gave me a stern look. "Not that I want to doubt your friend, but even the two of you are no match for the Manupian authorities if you get caught."

"I want to go back, Stephen. I want to find out what's going on." I remembered the face of the woman who attacked me out on the planet's surface and the anger as she raised the metal bar over her head. Followed by the terror when the Manupian security official ripped the mask from her face and she realised she was suffocating to death. "I want to know more about the workless."

"I don't know it's a good idea," said Stephen.

"You've agreed to pay my top rate, haven't you?"

"Yes, but–"

"Then it's a good idea. I'll meet up with Freddi and go back to Manupia. People will say a lot more to an ordinary person than they will to someone in a Fertillan Guard uniform. Don't worry, it'll be fine."

# Chapter Ten

THE BUILDING REACHED right up to the top of Londos, the main enclosed city on Fertilla. So high that it seemed not to have a roof at all, but to use the ceiling of the enclosure to top itself off. Each level had only two windows, but with eight levels, its sixteen windows suggested a lot of people worked there. A sign on the front, just above eye level, in simple black letters on white, read: Edsom's Exporters. It was an office building, almost certainly an administration centre for the food export industry. By the state of its grey facade, largely undamaged by the years of standing on a relatively busy street, it was obvious it was younger than many of the surrounding structures with their pock-marked surfaces which had suffered from various unknown knocks during the course of their lives.

I tried to remember the house that used to stand there, but it was lost somewhere in my memory. The only fragment that remained was a yellow door and my mother's hand on the keypad.

From the angle of the memory, I must have been very small because I seemed to be looking up. Although I would have been older than a baby because I think I was standing. I tried to extrapolate more from that fragment, but the harder I thought about it, the more it seemed to dissolve.

I took out my P-tab and brought up the photographs I had of my mother. Familiar images that were as much stored in my mind as they were in the electronic device in my hand. In them she was younger than the age I had become, but she had the same long dark hair and the same deep brown eyes. I stared at my most treasured photo of her for many minutes. She was smiling with my father on their wedding day at the start of what she must have thought would be a new chapter of her long life. But in a few years from that captured moment, she was to die in a fire that destroyed the house which once sat only a metre from my feet.

During the many minutes that I stood there, people walked by. One or two of them grumbled that I was in the way, but I had as much right to stand in the street as they had to walk in it. But I gradually became aware of a presence at my side. A presence who was neither grumbling nor passing by.

It was Freddi. Standing respectfully half a step back from me and, as always, with his face at the height of my shoulder.

"Freddi," I said. "What are you doing here?"

"Looking for you."

"How did you know I was here?"

"It's where you said you'd be in your last message. You'd meet me at Londos port to take the shuttle back to the ship, but you needed to go via Barkers Street first."

I didn't remember. I had been so distracted. "Of course."

"Thinking of going into the export business?" said Freddi, looking up at the sign on the building.

"What?" Then I realised. "Oh no. I used to live here. I wanted to come back to see it again. I didn't know they'd replaced the house with an office building."

"This is where your mother died?"

"Yeah." There was suddenly moisture in my eyes. Acknowledging it out loud brought back an emotion I thought I had extinguished long ago.

"You can't tell there was a fire here," said Freddi.

"People said I was lucky to be staying over at a friend's house when our place burnt down. But it meant I wasn't with her at the end."

"She would have preferred it that way," he said.

"I suppose."

"I don't remember you coming here before. Why now?"

"Something James said."

"Prince James?"

"Yeah. He said I should watch myself and think about what happened to my mother."

"What does that mean?"

"It was a threat, I think. He wanted something to hurt me and the only piece of information he could pull out of my file was that my mother died in a fire when I was a child."

"It was an empty threat," said Freddi. "He could only have been a child himself when it happened."

"I know that. But it made me think. I wanted to come back here to see it, even though there's nothing left of her or the house."

"Your memory is left. That's what's important. It's like, when

I come to Fertilla and go back to the farm and try not to have a blazing row with my daughters, I remember Ellen being there. It helps to let your feelings out, so you can put them away again."

He was right. I wiped the moisture from my eyes and put away the thoughts of my mother, like I had put away the pictures on my P-tab. "Come on, Freddi, let's get to the shuttle and back up to the ship."

"Where are we going?" he asked.

"Manupia," I said.

"The factory planet?"

I chuckled. Why was it that everybody said that? "Yeah, the factory planet."

We brought the shuttle down to Shangi port, the main space hub on the edge of Shangi, the largest of Manupia's industrial cities. Many of the products made in its factories left the planet at that point and many of the raw materials used in its manufacturing processes were offloaded there. It was an immense, sprawling, busy place which meant it was the most obvious jump-off point for a freelancer looking for work.

Not that that's what I was actually there for, but it made my cover story all the more believable.

I was so used to breathing in newly recycled air when arriving at an enclosed station of a planet, that the smell of the grime was the first thing I noticed when we disembarked. The mix of sweat, dirt and engine grease was almost as much part of the air as the oxygen and it had left its residue on every surface in the docking area. Everything was a shade of brown or grey, including the lighting which was kept subdued. On Fertilla, that would have indicated approaching evening, but in the Shangi port, it seemed to be the default. Ships big and small – from shuttles like our own to larger freight vessels – were lined up in a regimented pattern, while the crews that serviced them, and the cargo that was due to be loaded and unloaded was stacked up in piles everywhere. Between them moved the brown and grey grimy people, wheeled transport vehicles and heavy lifting machinery which bleeped a warning as they trundled along to indicate that the drivers couldn't easily see where they were going.

Freddi and I made our way through the dull environment, looking at each trader or contractor that we passed. Some of them looked back at us – mostly in a suspicious and unfriendly way – while the majority ignored us.

"We need to find a bar," said Freddi.

"Is everywhere we go about drinking beer for you?" I asked.

He frowned. "It's a good place to talk to the locals."

I certainly didn't fancy my chances of getting into a friendly conversation among all the cargo.

I jumped at the sound of a horn behind me and leapt out of the way of a wheeled lifter which had trundled towards us from out of nowhere. I nearly careered straight into a stack of containers almost as tall as I was and stood nervously as they wobbled with alarming instability. The lifter moved past us and, even though neither Freddi nor myself touched the stack, somehow the turbulence from the machinery caused enough disturbance for the top few containers to topple over.

Freddi pulled my arm and yanked me out of the way as they clattered to the ground at the very spot where I had been standing. Whatever metal pieces were inside them clanged together like the peal of broken bells.

"Hey!" called a gruff female voice from the other side of the toppled stack. "Get your hands off my cargo!"

I raised my hands up defensively. "I didn't touch them. It was the draught caused by the wheeled lifter."

"A draught? In here? Don't be a vac-arse!" She came round the other side of the stacks to reveal herself to be dressed in even darker colours than the grim shades of the rest of the docking area. The drabness of her clothes was made even more noticeable because she was topped off with a head of short, unkempt hair which she had bleached bright white.

"I'm sorry," I said. "There wasn't anything breakable in there?"

"Lucky for you, no," she said.

Freddi picked up the container nearest to him. "Here, why don't we help stack them up again?"

"If you're going to pick them up, you might as well carry them over to my ship," she said, pointing over at a cargo vessel about the same size as the personal spaceship on which I had first travelled to Manupia with Prince James.

Freddi turned, carrying the container which appeared to be of considerable weight, but only got as far as the bleach-haired woman before she put out a hand to stop him. He looked up at her like he was trying to fathom her problem. She looked back at him like there was something about his face that intrigued her. She stared at him for several, long moments.

"Freddi?" she said, eventually.

"Do I know you?"

"It's Patti!" she cried. She took the container from his hands and literally tossed it aside so it crashed to the floor. Then she put her arms around his waist, lifted him up and twirled him around so his legs swung out in a circle.

I stepped back to avoid being smacked in the face by his feet.

She came to a halt and set him back down again. "By the Deity, Freddi! You survived! You really made it."

Freddi's expression said his mind was catching up fast as recognition spread over his face. "Patti? I thought I'd never see you again. I assumed you were dead."

"If I'd have stayed, I probably would have been." She wiped her hand through her hair and left a grimy streak on its white strands. "Wow, Freddi. I'd say let's go for a beer, but I have all this stuff to get in the cargo hold."

"We'll help you," said Freddi.

"Really?" she said.

"It was sort of our fault it fell over in the first place."

It really wasn't, but I decided not to make a fuss and to introduce myself instead. "I'm Cassy. Freddi's captain."

She shook my hand dismissively and accepted my labour without gratitude. At least with the three of us, it didn't take long.

"I know a good bar not far from here," said Patti, when we had finished. "Well, 'good' might be overstating it, but it's not far at least. I assume you're paying?"

FREDDI AND PATTI sat on opposite sides of the small table in the crowded bar, drinking beer and laughing over old times. His eyes grew wide and bright in the dimness of the lighting as they recounted story after story telling how they had nearly died or nearly been caught back in the days when they had served on a pirate ship together. Their reminiscences sounded exciting and heroic. Not like the few stories he had shared with me in which life as a pirate sounded fairly horrific.

Patti, from what she was saying, had stayed with the pirates for a few years longer than Freddi before she was forced to get out. She said she had saved a bit of money – or stolen a bit of money, it wasn't clear – and set herself up with a spaceship of her own. She turned her back on a life of crime and opted to run a legitimate business, contracting for various operators out of Manupia. She claimed that a life on the straight and narrow was less exciting, but allowed her to sleep much better.

In theory, I was part of the conversation, but my presence at the table was of no more significance than the near-empty glasses which sat between us. I took to watching the other people sitting around us. It was the end of the day on Manupia and half the people from the docking area seemed to have congregated in the small bar, bringing their grimy smell with them. They were almost exclusively spacefarers and, as I tried to eavesdrop on their conversations, I found nothing to enlighten me about the situation on Manupia other than common complaints about low pay, tight schedules and unreasonable bosses.

Freddi finished up his second pint and slammed the glass down on the table where my elbow was resting. I was jolted away from my eavesdropping and back to the conversation which I had not been a part of.

"Want another one, Patti?" he said.

She looked at the dregs of her remaining beer and swirled them around in the bottom of her glass so they released the last of their bubbly fizz. "I'm supposed to be flying out of here tonight… but yeah, why not?"

"Cassy?" he offered, getting to his feet.

I had already eked out my first pint to avoid drinking another when Freddi went to the bar for a second round. If he was going to get drunk in that unfamiliar place, then I needed to stay relatively sober. "Not for me, thanks."

Freddi smiled at Patti as he went off to the bar for a refill.

It left us two women alone together and, after two pints, I figured Patti would be more willing to talk.

But it was her who got in the first question. "Are you and Freddi…?"

It caught me by surprise and I laughed. "Me and Freddi? No! He's part of my crew."

"Space can be lonely, though," said Patti. "I love being my own boss, but sometimes…"

I lifted up what was left of my beer. "I'll drink to that." I took a sip of the warm, bitter liquid, but only enough to taste it, not enough to feel the effects of its alcohol.

She drank the rest of her second pint. "So, what are you doing on Manupia?"

"Looking for work."

She dismissed the suggestion. "There's precious little here for freelancers. Even the work there used to be has dried up."

"Oh?" I prompted.

"Their factories are inefficient compared to some of the new players out there in the Rim. It's forcing them to produce less and there's less for the workforce to do."

"I'd like to see inside their factories," I said. "I hear the Jonsonii factory is the one to see."

"Ah." Patti leant back in her chair and nodded like it was all becoming clear. She went to drink more of her beer, then realised it was empty. "Now it makes sense why two people from Fertilla are here. It's because of the Fertillan prince."

I went hot. There was no way she could know about that. *No way.* I brought my beer to my lips and hoped the glass hid some of the redness I felt rushing to my cheeks. "The Fertillan prince?"

"Prince James will be visiting the Jonsonii factory soon, but you probably already know that. You're lucky actually, he was due to visit last week, but it was postponed for some reason."

"I thought that sort of information was supposed to be kept secret."

"Kept secret from most people, yes." Patti grinned. "But I'm not most people."

Freddi returned from the bar with two pints. The glasses were both full to the brim and Patti's spilled a little over the edge as he put it in front of her. He took a slurp from his own glass and sat back down again.

"Cassy's been telling me she's interested in seeing inside Shangi's main factory," said Patti.

"So you weren't talking about me, then?" he said.

I rolled my eyes. "Sometimes, Freddi, two women are able to have a conversation that isn't about you."

He grinned nevertheless and drank his beer.

"It's impossible anyway," said Patti. "The factory's locked down. Workers only and strictly no visitors. Unless you happen to be a member of a royal family, and even then President Udinov has to sign it off."

I sat back in my chair. It didn't sound like it was going to be easy.

"Why?" said Freddi. "It's a factory, it's not like they're making secret weapons in there… unless they are."

"Industrial espionage," said Patti, as if that explained everything.

Both of us stared blankly at her.

"They're terrified of manufacturing details being stolen," she explained. "Say, for example, they make some kind of vital engine part for a spaceship. A spy comes along, steals the plans for that part, takes it to another planet and suddenly this other planet has the means to make the engine part. If they can do it cheaper, buyers stop coming to Manupia and Manupia's in trouble."

"I'm not a spy," I said. Well, I was, but not an industrial one. "I just want to know what Prince James is up to. To do that, I need to get into the Jonsonii factory. There must be a way."

Patti traced her finger around the rim of her beer glass in thought. "I may be able to help. For a price."

I leant across the table and kept my voice low. "I'm interested."

Patti did the same. "Getting into the factory when you don't work there – without breaking in and causing a scene, of course – is virtually impossible. The answer, therefore, is to become one of the workforce."

"You can get me job?" I said.

"Not exactly," said Patti. "Manupia used to be a planet where no one was out of work, but not recently. I don't know if you've heard of the workless."

"Let's say that we've met," I said.

"Which means getting a job on this planet has become a lot harder, and it would be virtually impossible for an off-worlder to secure a position."

"I thought you said you could get me in."

"You have to take the place of one of the existing workers by taking on their identity. I happen to know a few people who are leaving the planet before the situation here gets worse and I could arrange for you to take the place of one of them. It's not cheap, however, as clearly the other workers will know you aren't that person and will need to be bribed."

"Not to mention you'll be taking your cut," Freddi suggested.

"Naturally," said Patti.

I didn't much care. Stephen was paying. "Do you know when Prince James is coming?"

"No, but from the talk I hear, I would expect him within the next week. I can get you in the factory before then, but you may have to do a few days' work before he arrives. How are you at factory work, Cassy?"

I thought about it. Terrible, probably. "I'll let you know afterwards."

# CHAPTER ELEVEN

THE TRANSPORTS AND freight ships were silent. The men and the women who loaded and unloaded their cargo were locked inside for the Manupian night. Surrounding the ships sat crates of raw materials ready to be moved out in the morning to serve the factories of Manupia. Above, in the artificial sky that enclosed the docking area, dim lights barely glowed, like dying stars casting soft and eerie shadows on the grimy floor around us.

Patti, Freddi and myself stood in the shadow of a large freighter. Waiting.

The shuffle of tentative footsteps brushed through the silence and I peered further into the twilight.

Emerging from behind a crate as tall as she was, stepped a woman. Her face was hidden in shadow, but her nervousness showed in the way she clutched hold of the bag that hung from her shoulder. "Hello?" she called, quietly and cautiously.

Patti broke away from our hiding place and stepped out into full view. I followed, with Freddi at my side.

The woman seemed to gain confidence and stood tall to face us. She was older than me, in her midlife, with short, scruffy brown hair kept back from her face by a band of bright blue material. She wore bib and braces overalls of a more sombre blue and stood with her hands plunged deep into two generous pockets at her hips.

"Hello, Mel," said Patti. "Is everything arranged?"

"It is," said Mel.

"This is the person who you will be taking into the factory." Patti nodded across at me.

I felt a sudden trepidation like I was about embark on something very dangerous when, in fact, I was only becoming part of an ordinary workforce for a brief period of time. I had taken on freelance jobs much more dangerous than that. And yet, the feeling persisted.

"Do you have the payment?" Mel asked.

Patti reached into the pocket of her jacket and pulled out a bulging, brown envelope and offered it to Mel, who snatched it from her, peered inside, seemed satisfied, re-sealed the envelope and stuffed it into the pocket of her overalls.

Only then did she look across at me. "Done any factory work before?"

"No," I said.

She frowned. "Even more important that you listen to what I say, do what I tell you to do and keep your head down. Understand? Mistakes can get you dead."

"I understand," I said.

Freddi leant in close to me. "Are you sure you want to do this?"

"Have you got a better plan?"

"Go back to the ship, fly off and find a proper freelance job."

"You back out now," said Mel, "and I keep the payment. Making arrangements doesn't come cheap."

"I'm not backing out," I said, firmly. I took out my P-tab, with everything that could identify me – my official ID, my money, my messages – and held it up to show her before I passed it to Freddi for safe-keeping.

Mel looked down at where my EE weapon was strapped to my thigh. "You can't take that either."

I reached down for it, gripped the handle and savoured the feeling of protection it gave me. Then I pulled it out of its holster and gave it to Freddi. He took it, but gave me a doubtful look as if to say he still wasn't happy about the idea.

"And the holster," said Mel.

I unbuckled it from my waist and undid the strap around my leg. This, too, I passed to Freddi.

"Better," she said. "Now put these on."

She threw her shoulder bag across to me. Inside, I found a set of bib and braces overalls, a drab brown shirt and a hairband similar to the one she wore, but in black. I changed behind a crate and emerged in the drab clothing, with my hair swept back from my face. Like with the Fertillan Guard uniform I had worn, I felt the disguise chip away at my personality. All the external things that reflected who I was were stripped away: my gun, my long flowing hair, my clothes.

Mel snatched the bag into which I had placed my own clothes and passed it to Freddi. She pulled out an elastic band from a side pocket and offered it to me. "Tie your hair back completely," she said. "I've seen women get their hair caught in factory machinery. They live to regret it, but not for very long."

I did as I was told. My disguise was complete and my identity hidden.

"Now you're ready to do some real work," she said.

A noise, like someone dropping something made of metal, rang out from somewhere among the other freighters. Mel flinched. Patti withdrew into the shadows.

Twilight was receding and the docking area was starting to wake.

"Come on," said Mel. "Being late will attract attention."

I followed Mel out of the docking area.

"Meet you in the bar in two days," Freddi called out as we left.

I turned to acknowledge him, only to see Patti pull him away from me and back into the shadows.

My undercover name was Sheri. The woman whose name I was using had left the planet for the promise of better and more secure work elsewhere. It was something the supposedly dedicated factory workers were not supposed to do and so she left under a veil of secrecy. It meant her employment had not been officially terminated and so her security pass, which Mel handed to me, should have been enough to get me in and out of the Jonsonii factory.

The only way to the centre of Shangi for pedestrians was via public transport, a pressurised tube-like train which ran the short distance across the Manupian wasteland to a transport station inside the city itself. From there, we walked to the factory. It was a long walk – more than a person who lived on a spaceship was used to – and I was tired before I had even begun the day's work.

The building was monstrous: an immense facade of black that rose up to the full height of the artificial sky and spread twice as wide. It not only marked the end of the street, it *was* the end of the street. The city stopped at the threshold to the Jonsonii factory – whatever lay beyond its giant vehicle-sized double doors appeared to be built directly out onto the planet's surface. It was, it seemed, its own enclosed, environmentally controlled space.

The workers entered via a more human-sized door and were scanned in, one by one. Mel and I made it, breathless, to the back of the queue of the last couple of stragglers arriving for work and I held my pass out ready in my sweaty hand.

The person in front of me tapped their pass on a reader. A red indicator light turned green, the door swung open, the person entered and the door closed again.

Mel stepped back. "Now you," she said.

I tapped the pass that belonged to another woman and stared nervously at the red light. It turned green. It let me in.

Entering the Jonsonii factory was like entering another city. If there was a back wall to the building, I couldn't see it from where I was standing as the walls and ceiling stretched back to a horizon obscured by machinery. The machines hung down from above, they grew out of the floor and they groaned and hissed with the movement of joints and firing of pistons. Within the rows and rows of assembly lines stood the people who worked there, dwarfed by the equipment they served. I breathed in a mouthful of air, heavy with humidity, and tasted the tang of metal mixed with the smell of human sweat.

I was standing just inside the doorway as Mel came in behind me and almost bumped into me. "This way."

She led me into the heart of the building. As I got closer to the individual workstations, I got more of a sense of what they were all doing. Throughout the vast building, the people and machines appeared to be making metal components for other machines. Some of the pieces wouldn't have looked out of place in my spaceship, while most served no obvious purpose on their own and were probably components for something much larger. Each piece was processed, put into boxes and transported away to wherever they were destined to go.

I was put on a workstation next to Mel's where my job was to finish a consignment of metal components which Mel described as 'widgets'. They were flat, about the depth of my little finger, and elbow-shaped with bolt holes at either end to secure them to something else. I had to check each one for faults, drill out any of the bolt holes which weren't clean cut and smooth down any rough edges with a deburring machine. I had a pair of thick gloves to protect my hands and a pair of goggles to protect my eyes. It made me appreciate Mel's warning about my hair. The drill was scary enough, with its twirling bit that I had to thread through the holes, but the deburring machine with its spinning wheel of industrial diamonds looked like it could burrow through flesh.

One man walked among all the workers to check we were carrying out our tasks with the expected quality and proficiency. His name, I learnt, was Grundor and he considered himself superior to the other workers, even though he was indentured to his employer just the same as the rest. My hand shook with nerves as he approached my workstation for the first time, and I had to stop deburring the piece of metal I was working on while I steadied myself. It was soon obvious he was one of the people who had been bribed to keep his mouth shut about my clandestine appearance on the factory floor.

"This must be 'Sheri'," he said, putting an emphasis on my undercover name to show he knew it was false. "How are you finding your work, 'Sheri'?"

I didn't look at him. "Can't complain," I said, examining the elbow-shaped piece of metal in my hand, even though I had already examined it.

"Exactly right," he said. He gave Mel a knowing wink before walking away and going to bother someone else.

If he was one of the people I was relying on to not to give me away, I was going to have to be more careful than I thought. I threw a glance over to Mel, but she shook her head to suggest I should say nothing, and went back to attending to her own widgets.

It was a long, gruelling, monotonous shift and by the time we were offered a break, my back was aching from standing for so long and my legs had gone numb. The pleasure at being able to walk away from my station was only matched by the pain in my body from having to move. None of the other workers seemed to be affected as we all moved, in an ever-increasing swarm, towards a set of steps which led to an upper floor. Either their bodies had built up the required strength for the work they were doing, or they had grown accustomed to ignoring the number of aches I assumed they all must have.

The volume of talking people around me grew into a babble as we congregated into one mass going up the stairs. One word seemed to be common to every conversation: 'coffee'.

"I'm dying for a coffee," said Mel as she joined me on the stairs.

After my first session at the machine, I could do with a caffeine hit myself.

The level above the factory floor consisted mostly of a massive room with rows of tables and chairs and a lengthy queue to collect food from a serving station along the nearside wall. Lunch options were either brownish soup with a bread roll or reddish soup with a bread roll. I opted for red and followed Mel to sit at one of the tables.

"How's it going?" asked Mel.

"I'm getting the hang of it," I said. Then I leant forward and whispered: "No one seems to have noticed me."

She shrugged. "You're not the first to come in on someone else's pass."

"Oh?" I took a sip of my soup and tasted its sweet tomatoness.

Mel dipped her roll into her brown soup and let the end of it drip back into the bowl before putting the whole soggy piece into her mouth. She chewed and swallowed before answering me. "Some people are leaving Manupia for the promise of new jobs and new opportunities in other parts of the Obsidian Rim. When they go, they leave behind a vacancy and where there's a vacancy, there's a horde of workless willing to take their place. They're so desperate, they'll work for nothing but soup and coffee until those in charge have syphoned off enough of their wages to satisfy whatever they consider a fair price for getting them the job. Then the records are changed behind the scenes and they become employed here in their own right."

That explained Grundor's behaviour on the factory floor. He may have taken a bribe to smooth things over officially, but there was no need to keep quiet when everyone knew what was going on.

An excited murmur went around the crowd of factory workers and, again, the word 'coffee' emanated from all around me. Grundor and a stream of others came out from behind the serving station, each carrying two large insulated jugs which they paraded around the tables, filling the cups of the seated masses with steaming black liquid. Its seductive smell soon filled the room and I found myself anticipating drinking my own small cup of the stuff.

Coffee was variously available in different places around the galaxy. I had drunk it on occasion and found it to be an acquired taste which I never had the money to acquire. Clean, fresh water was expensive enough and when we wanted to relax with a drink, Freddi would always opt for beer and I was always happy to join him.

Grundor got closer and I pushed my empty cup to the edge of the table for filling. But after Grundor filled Mel's cup, he paused. "I see we have a new girl."

The tomato soup and bread I was digesting stirred uncomfortably in my stomach. I quickly glanced around and realised there were, maybe, fifty factory workers between me and the way out if I needed to make a run for it. Instinctively, I clutched at my thigh where I usually kept my personal EE weapon, but all that I touched was the fabric of my overalls covering my bare leg.

Grundor waved at someone near the service station and they ran off through the door to what I assumed to be the kitchen.

"On your feet, new girl!" bellowed Grundor.

The hubbub in the canteen quietened and the factory workers turned to look at me. If I had next to zero chance of making an escape before, then the odds had just crashed into the minus.

I looked across to Mel for help, but she sat back in her chair and folded her arms. It was then that I realised my folly in paying everyone upfront. Whatever happened to me from there on in, they would get their money regardless.

"On your feet!" bellowed Grundor again. I was shuffling to prise myself off my chair when he grabbed my sleeve and pulled me to standing.

A chant started behind me. "*Fight! Fight!*" they seemed to be saying. It radiated out from where it started like the ripples of an explosion until everyone around me was demanding: "*Fight! Fight!*"

Mel was grinning and stamping her foot in time to the rhythm.

So this was it, I was going to die in a factory brawl on an alien planet under an assumed name.

The person who had run behind into the kitchen came back out holding a large ceramic mug, as big as a beer glass, which he brought directly to Grundor.

I felt myself blush as I realised the people around were not chanting 'fight', but 'pint'.

"*Pint! Pint! Pint!*" they chanted as Grundor took the mug, placed it on the table and filled it with steaming black liquid.

He said quietly to me: "You must drink it all in one go or they won't be satisfied."

Mel nodded as I picked up the mug by its handle. The rich smell of coffee was intoxicating. The workers clapped their hands in time with the rhythm of their chant: "*Pint! Pint! Pint!*"

I bought the mug to my lips – hoping the liquid wasn't too hot – and drank.

Gulp after gulp – "*Pint! Pint!*" – barely tasting as I swallowed and breathed, swallowed and breathed, feeling it burn my throat with its heat and its dark sweetness until it was all gone. I pulled the mug from my lips and everyone around me thumped their feet on the floor rapidly like the beat of heavy rain on the shelter of a planet with clouds.

Grundor snatched the mug from my hand and held it above his head. The rumble of feet intensified. He turned the mug upside down and the minutest drip of coffee fell to the floor. The place erupted into a cheer.

Only for a moment and then their entertainment was over.

Heads turned away from me, one by one, as I ceased to be of interest and they went back to their own meals. Grundor continued on his rounds, delivering more modest cups of coffee to the people who were still waiting.

I flopped back in my chair in somewhat of a daze. "What the vac was that?" I said.

"Your initiation," said Mel. "Congratulations, you're now one of the Jonsonii factory workers."

# Chapter Twelve

I WAS WIRED FOR the rest of the shift. I was buzzing so much I had to force myself to concentrate to not drill a hole in my hand instead of one of the elbow-shaped pieces of metal. Even so, the lift the coffee gave me helped me get through the day and forget my aching back and legs. I could see why it was so much the topic of conversation when people took their break, although I wish I hadn't drunk a whole pint of the stuff.

As we left, Grundor and several helpers stood by the door and handed out little sachets to everyone. I looked curiously at mine: it was about half the size of my palm and rattled when I shook it.

"What's this?" I said, holding it up to the light to see if I could see through the small, sealed envelope.

"Dried coffee," said Mel.

"What for?"

"You put it in hot water and drink it before work. Trust me, in the morning, you'll want it."

"If you say so." I stuffed it in my overalls pocket.

When we emerged into the street, the noise of the factory was replaced with people shouting. There weren't many of them, perhaps around twenty, but they yelled louder when they saw us:

"*Give us jobs! … We can work! … What gives* you *the right to work when we don't?*"

I glanced round to see red, angry faces peering out from a mob of brown clothing. Men, women, some almost young enough to be children, and a few older and frail. Some of the workless. Not as desperate as the people who attacked our car out in the wasteland, maybe, but not far from it. They were being held back by five men in the black uniform of Manupian security. Their faces leant through the gaps between the security barrier created by the linked arms of the officials and stared at us with jealousy.

"*Jobs! Jobs! Jobs!*"

Mel pulled me away from them and hurried down the street.

I said nothing. She said nothing. She ignored them like they weren't there. It was like they were non-people.

As we walked, and the chants of the workless became distant, I got the feeling that someone was following us. I slowed my pace and listened to the footsteps closing in.

I stopped suddenly and turned. The woman behind us – a factory worker – jumped almost out of her skin and yelped.

Mel turned also. "Denni, what are you doing?"

"I…" The woman, petite, timid and much younger than the two of us, looked at me uncertainly.

"Don't worry about her," said Mel.

But still, Denni leant towards Mel and whispered, "I have the money."

"Are you sure?" said Mel.

"You can look at my account if you want." Denni pulled a P-tab from her pocket.

But Mel waved it away. "That's not what I meant. Are you sure you want to leave? It's tomorrow night."

"I'm too young to be workless, Mel."

"They're not going to make you workless, Denni. Not someone like you."

"You don't know that!"

Mel turned to me. "You go on ahead, I'll catch you up."

I tried to protest, but she was having none of it.

"I won't be long."

It was agreed that I should stay at Mel's home during my undercover operation rather than risk drawing attention by taking a transport to the docking area to sleep in the shuttle. Except, I had no idea where Mel's home actually was. So I walked down the street enough to give her privacy and waited for her there.

Looking back, I saw what on any other part of the Obsidian Rim might have been a drug deal going down. Both Mel and Denni huddled close to each other to hide the exchange on their P-tabs. Then they parted and walked in different directions as if they didn't know each other at all.

Mel's expression was impassive as she came towards me, but we both knew what she had been up to. It made sense that Mel was the one arranging for people to get off Manupia. She must have arranged for Sheri to leave, which was why she was able to give Sheri's security pass to me.

Mel lived in a row of identical houses that lined one of the identical residential streets of Manupia's largest city.

There were no gaps between the houses, it was one long wall with doors and windows spaced at regular intervals to form a snaking terrace. The only way to distinguish each dwelling from the other was the colour of the door and a number stencilled at eye level. Mel stopped at a dark blue door with a number 185 and let us in.

It was only then that I saw that the 'house' was actually two dwellings. One was accessed at the top of a set of narrow stairs directly inside the door, and the other – Mel's home – was through a second door on the right. On other planets where people lived in an assigned complex inside a single structure, people referred to living in 'apartments'. On Manupia, it seemed, they were called 'flats'. It was an apt description for a dwelling which was on one level – street level – with no stairs up or down.

Everything in it was brown, casting a sepia tone across the whole of her living space. Mel led me into a small sitting room which had a hard floor softened with a faded rug and plain walls devoid of decoration. The only splash of colour was in the face of an old man sitting in one of the frayed fabric-covered brown chairs.

"Hello, Dad," said Mel as she entered. "This is my friend Sheri."

I stood in the doorway as he narrowed his eyes to stare at me.

"Don't you have another friend called Sheri?" he said in a throaty voice which sounded like it had degraded with age.

"It's complicated," replied Mel. She pulled Patti's envelope from her deep overall pocket and took it over to him.

He opened the envelope and he peered in. "Ooh, coffee!" He made a play of rubbing his hands together while licking his lips.

"I'll make you some," said Mel and she went through another door at the far end of the room, leaving me alone with her father.

"Come in, come in." He gestured me forward with an impatient wave of his hand. "Sit! Sit!"

I sat down in one of the worn chairs as the seductive smell of coffee filtered into the room. Mel's father smelt it too and his eyes widened with anticipation. Mel returned with a small cup about half the size of the ones the workers had drunk from at the factory.

"Ooh, lovely!"

"Careful, it's hot!" she said.

He frowned at her and restricted himself to taking in the aroma by holding his nose a fraction above the rim of the cup. "Old codgers like me used to be able to take on smaller jobs to keep us busy and keep us in coffee as we got less able," he said. "But now they would rather get rid of us and I'm forced to rely on my daughter for coffee."

"Our guest doesn't want to listen to politics," said Mel.

"I don't mind," I said.

"I keep telling Melarny to get out while she can. Leave me, find new opportunities – find a man, even. But she's stubborn."

"Dad, let's not talk about this now."

"Why not now?"

"We have a guest." She threw her gaze across to me and then stared pointedly at her father.

"Perhaps our guest can talk some sense into you."

"*Dad!*" Mel scowled at him.

"I'm just saying, don't waste your whole life looking after me."

"It's not a waste, Dad," she said. "You drink that while I make dinner."

She went back through the internal door which, I assumed, led to the kitchen.

The old man took a grateful sip of his coffee, savouring the liquid for a moment before closing his eyes and swallowing. When he opened his eyes again, it was to stare right at me. "Melarny's a good child, but she let herself get sucked in," he said, leaning forward and lowering his voice to a whisper. "You may feel privileged to secure yourself a job working in the factory, but I'm warning you not to let yourself get sucked in. The factory feels like your family, but they are really your masters. You give them your loyalty, you give them your life and then they spit you out again like a lump of mouldy bread. They will own you and, when they have taken everything from you that they can, they will throw you away."

He said nothing else to me after that. He merely drank his coffee, eking it out until Mel brought dinner for the three of us and the conversation turned to trivial things.

I UNDERSTOOD WHAT Mel's father meant about the factory being like a family. The next day, no one looked at me like an outsider. I became accepted as one of the workers and, when we broke for lunch, we all sat around talking and laughing until the signal came to return to the machines.

The work itself was hard and monotonous, but to feel I was part of something with thousands of other people within the Jonsonii factory gave me a sense of pride and I actually started to enjoy the work itself. I took to counting the number of metal elbows that passed through my hands and set myself targets to overcome.

I never thought life on a planet could compete with being in space, but somehow it did.

After two days, I finished my shift and walked straight past the workless without hearing the things they shouted. It was sad for them, but I came to regard them as outsiders while their shouts of anger became part of the ambient noise of the street. It was the day I had promised to meet Freddi and, although I wanted to go back to Mel's home to rest, I honoured my promise and took a transport to the docking area where I was able to find my way to the bar.

Before entering, I let down my hair and shook it out so it fell over my shoulders and unclipped the bib of my overalls, so it hung down at my waist and revealed my shirt underneath. I hoped it was enough to make me look less like a factory worker.

I found Freddi and Patti sitting closely around the same table where we had sat before, each with a half-drunk pint of beer in front of them. I swear I saw them sit back in their seats when they noticed me coming round the corner. Patti ran a hand nonchalantly through her bleached blond hair and I got the feeling that neither of them had wanted me to see how close they had been.

"Hey, Cassy!" said Freddi with uncharacteristic enthusiasm. "How about a drink?"

Without waiting for an answer, he was on his feet and heading across to the bar.

I sat down and Patti acknowledged my presence with a smile.

"I'm glad you've come," she said. "I have some news about Prince James."

"Oh?" I expected to be excited, or at the very least curious, but somehow I wasn't.

"He's on Manupia," said Patti. "Looks like he'll be staying the night and touring the factory tomorrow."

"The Jonsonii factory? Are you sure? I've heard nothing on the factory floor."

"That's my information. It's one of the biggest factories on Manupia and the easiest to get to from headquarters, so it makes sense."

"When you say, 'touring the factory'…?"

"That's all I know. He could walk around and talk to the workers, he could slip in through the back and disappear into a back room where you won't see him. He could do both, he could do neither."

"How am I supposed to come up with a plan to find out what he's up to?"

"That's up to you," said Patti. "I wasn't paid to come up with a plan. Plans cost extra."

Freddi returned from the bar carrying three pints: one in each hand and a third wedged precariously between the other two. I took the third one from him before he either dropped it or spilled it on me.

"What's it like working at the factory?" said Freddi, handing out the remaining pints to himself and Patti.

"Pretty good, actually," I said.

He laughed and downed the last of his previous pint of beer which he had left on the table.

"No really," I said. "The camaraderie of the place is amazing. We have a laugh and a joke and we have competitions to see how much work we can get through in a session. It's fun."

He stared at me with wide eyes, holding his empty glass in front of him like he had forgotten to put it down. "Fun?"

"It's lonely out in space. Sometimes it's nice to be with people."

Freddi looked across to Patti. "Is she joking? While I was at the bar, did you two plan to wind me up?"

"She's gone native," said Patti.

"I haven't!"

Patti didn't even look at me. "There's a reason why Manupia has a reputation for having a strong work ethic."

Freddi reached out his hand and clasped it around my fingers. "Are you all right, Cassy?" It was an unexpected and unusual sign of affection from him. Its warmth ran through my body as I felt the chill of Patti's gaze as she looked at where our hands touched.

"I'm fine, Freddi." I pulled away from him, but he kept his concerned look.

"You better drink up that beer," Patti told me. "You need to take a transport back to the centre of town before they stop running. We should also limit the time you're seen talking to us."

I drank the beer, but I didn't enjoy it.

Our meeting was supposed to be about me and my mission, but I felt like a gatecrasher. I barely even had time to metabolise the alcohol before I got up to go.

"Meet you back here again at this time tomorrow," said Freddi, looking around to check no one was listening. "Assuming you get what you came for."

"If the tour happens as you say," I said.

"It'll happen," said Patti.

"I almost forgot," said Freddi, pulling a P-tab from his trouser pocket.

He stood up, grabbed my hand and pressed the gadget into my palm. "It's a new one. No data. No identifying markers.

Use it to communicate with me. We'll be here at this time tomorrow. If you don't show and I don't hear from you, I'll come looking."

"Freddi, what are you concerned about?"

"Nothing, Cassy. You said you're fine and I believe you."

I secreted the P-tab in my pocket and turned to leave. At the last minute, I decided to take advantage of the bar's toilet facilities before making the journey back to Mel's flat. As I left, I saw Freddi and Patti – unaware I was watching them – laughing and joking together like they had never been apart. It was good to see him happy, but it gave me an uncomfortable feeling.

# Chapter Thirteen

**A**WHISPER WENT ROUND the factory floor that the President of Manupia was in the building.

It shouldn't have been possible to hear a whisper over the noise of the machinery, but the hushed excitement of thousands of workers somehow transcended the cacophony of working machines and swept through the air where it created an excited buzz in the atmosphere.

Heads turned, ever so subtly, and eyes glanced from behind workstations towards the factory's main entrance. I followed their example to see President Udinov being led by a very pleased-with-himself Grundor onto the factory floor, with Prince James behind and a following entourage of two Fertillan Guards and two Manupian security officials.

Patti's information was right. I tensed with anxiety. It was time to do what I came to Manupia to do, although how I was going to do it, I didn't know.

The spinning wheel of my deburring machine tugged at my glove. In a moment's inattention, I had let my hand drift towards the machine. I yanked it back and looked at where the industrial diamonds had worn a hole in the fabric. I went hot at the thought of how close I had come to losing my fingers. I switched off the wheel and glanced over to where the delegation were making their way down one of the rows of workers. They were talking to each other, but I was too far away, and the factory was too noisy, to hear what they were saying.

I leant across my workstation towards Mel. "What do you think they're doing?"

She pushed a thick piece of material under the gnashing cutting arm of her machine. It chomped at the material with hungry teeth. "Is that Prince James with President Udinov?"

"Yes."

She peered over the heads of her fellow workers. "Looks like they're taking a tour."

"I need to find out why," I said.

"There's a meeting room upstairs by the canteen. I imagine they'll discuss it in there."

That was all I needed to hear. I pulled off my gloves and took off my goggles.

"What are you doing?" said Mel.

"Cover for me."

"No!" she said, as I crouched down to make myself less conspicuous and scurried down the row of workers. Everyone else either had their attention on their work or were looking at President Udinov. So I was able to reach the door and slip through to the stairs unnoticed.

I had never paid attention to the second door which led off the landing at the top of the stairs before. In the few days I had been working there, I had always been propelled into the canteen by the momentum of the other workers hungry for soup and coffee. This time there was only me at the top of the stairs and a stern-looking Manupian security officer standing in front of the second door which Mel said led to a meeting room. As I looked at the sidearm strapped to his thigh, I felt him staring at me and knew I wasn't going to get through that door without a good excuse or an EEW – neither of which I had.

Feeling the security official's stare intensify, I turned to the canteen, as if I had intended to go in there all along. But someone was coming out at the same time and I nearly walked straight into her. The young woman, who wore a white catering tunic and trousers, was carrying a tray of neatly cut sandwiches with bread so fresh that the smell made my stomach rumble. She stopped suddenly when she saw me and the tray tipped sideways. Its yummy contents almost went tumbling to the floor, but somehow she managed to stabilise it and disaster was averted.

"Careful!"

"Sorry," I said.

She grimaced and carried her tray up to the security official. He opened the door which led to the meeting room and she went through with a polite, 'thank you'.

Realising I had just witnessed an example of a good excuse, I hurried into the canteen.

The room was big and echoey without a horde of workers inside of it and I felt very conspicuous. I looked across to where the entrance to the kitchen lay behind the serving area and dashed over to it.

The door to the kitchen could be pushed open from either direction and had a round porthole set at eye level to allow people to see through to the other side. Its purpose, I was sure, was to avoid a clash like the one I had nearly had with the tray of sandwiches. The other advantage of the porthole was that I could check if the coast was clear before I went in.

No such luck. There was a man in catering whites inside. He was facing away from me at the sink which ran along the back wall of the kitchen. Not that it was like any kitchen I had ever been in. Everything was so much bigger. The worktops were long and spartan with an array of large pans and cooking utensils hanging from hooks above them. There were three oversize ovens, the massive sink, and a fridge so large that it looked like several people could fit inside it.

The man turned round holding a jug of water and I pulled myself back from the porthole. I pressed my back against the wall by the door and tried to come up with a plan. Attacking the man, knocking him out and stealing his uniform would cause too much noise and attract attention. Threatening to kill him, making him strip, tying him up and shutting him in a cupboard was too complicated and fraught with opportunities to go wrong. Besides, I didn't have a gun and the only knives available to threaten him with were hanging up above the worktops – closer to him than they were to me.

I took another quick peek through the porthole. The man had placed the jug on a tray with a collection of glasses which he picked up and began to carry towards the door.

I ducked out of sight again as a plan formed in my mind.

I counted the number of steps he would need to take to get to the door and, at the right point, I pushed hard from my side.

The door swung into the kitchen and slammed against the tray in his hand. The tray tipped up, the jug fell backwards and poured water over his chest and down his body.

"Drakh!" he yelled as he dropped the whole thing and the jug, glasses and the tray itself tumbled to the ground in a cascade of clangs and smashes.

"Oh my Deity!" I said in feigned shock as I came right into the kitchen. "I'm *so* sorry."

He stood in a pool of spilt water and broken glass, with droplets falling from his sodden uniform. His tunic was so wet, I could see his brown undershirt beneath.

"What the vac are you doing?" he yelled at me.

"I came to see if I could get some coffee ahead of the break." It was a lame excuse, but by the way the workers talked about coffee, it was a believable one.

"No one's allowed coffee outside of break, you vackless vacbrain!" He shook his arms and drips of water flew off the ends. One went into my eye. I blinked it away.

"Let me help clear that up," I said, and bent down to pick up the few surviving glasses which I placed on the tray. "Do you have any more catering clothes?"

"In my locker," he grumbled.

"That's good," I said, trying not to sound too pleased.

He grumbled again and walked to the other end of the kitchen where there was a rack of tall, thin cupboards; squelching as he left watery footprints on the shiny floor. I made play of doing a bit more clearing up by picking up the jug and putting both it and the tray on the worktop.

His locker was in the middle of the row and activated by a combination which I was too far away to see him type in. The tiny whir of a motor sounded and the door clicked open. Hanging up inside was one single set of catering whites. He took them out, pushed the door shut again, the lock whirred to secure it and he plodded back towards me.

"Where are you going?" I asked, as he headed for the door.

"To the toilets to dry off and change," he said. "You didn't expect me to strip off in the kitchen, did you?"

I kind of did. I kind of hoped he would either show me where they kept all the catering uniforms so I could steal one, or he would take off his wet clothes which I could steal with the idea that a damp disguise was better than none.

"I feel really bad," I said. "I'll mop up the water and the glass while you're gone."

"Yeah, do that," he said. "But don't think you're getting any coffee. I've got enough going on today without dealing with vackless staff in coffee withdrawal."

He left. I had precious minutes. I grabbed a large knife from above the worktop and hurried over to the array of lockers. If one of them contained a spare catering uniform, then it made sense that the others did as well.

I slid the knife between the door and the frame of the first locker and felt the blade strike the hard metal bolt that kept it locked shut. I tried to slip the knife around the bolt, but it was solid and inserted further into the frame than I could reach with the makeshift tool. It gave me enough information, however, to realise the locker was secured with a single bolt. I also realised that the doors were made of thin, potentially bendable metal.

It was a system designed to deter casual, opportunistic thieves, not desperate and determined ones. So I slid my knife in again, but this time at the bottom. It gave me just enough purchase to bend the bottom corner and grab hold of it. I dropped the knife, pulled at the metal and managed to peel it open to create a gap big enough to get my hand inside.

To my excitement, I could see the white of clothing through the hole. It was hanging from a hanger or hook inside. Pushing my arm in as far as I could, I ran my hand up the fabric until I could reach no more. Not far enough to get to wherever it was secured. So I tugged it gently. I tugged it again. I yanked it as hard as I could and, with an alarming sound of ripping material, the clothes came free and I pulled them out through the hole.

There was a nasty rip in the collar of the tunic and on the waistband of the trousers, but I could get away with that. The first I could hide with my hair and the second would be hidden by the length of the tunic itself.

I threw off my overalls and retrieved my security pass and the P-tab Freddi had given me from the pockets. Hoping the man I'd soaked to the skin was still drying himself off in the toilets, I stuffed my overalls inside the locker and secreted the pass and P-tab into my crop-top bra. I put on the white uniform. It was a bit big for me, but it didn't entirely fall off and would have to do. I pulled off the headband which held back my hair and rearranged it into a quick ponytail. It was a makeshift disguise, but it only needed to fool Manupian security at a glance.

The tray was waiting for me, where I'd left it, on the side. The four surviving glasses would have to be enough, but the empty jug could give me away. I risked valuable seconds to fill it at the sink.

"Come on, come on, come on," I urged the tap as it took its own sweet time filling the jug with water. When it was three-quarters full, I shut off the tap and took the jug to my completed tray. I picked it up and stepped back out into the empty canteen.

As the kitchen door closed behind me, the door to the entrance by the stairs pushed open.

I caught only the flash of white clothing before I ducked down behind the serving area. I held my breath.

It had to be the woman I had seen earlier. In the haste of making my plan, I had forgotten about her. I listened to her soft footsteps as she came closer, went past and into the kitchen. I bobbed up from my hiding place, only to see the door to the staff toilets at the back of the room open. I ducked down again and listened to heavier footsteps of the man walk past me, followed by him pushing open the kitchen door with a hard shove.

Inside, he would see that I hadn't mopped up the spilled water and broken glass like I had said. If both of them looked across at the lockers, they would see the door to one of them bent back on itself and the gaping hole I had left.

Knowing I was now on borrowed time, I came out from my hiding place and headed for the landing where I would have to test my disguise against the professionalism, or otherwise, of the Manupian security official.

# CHAPTER FOURTEEN

THE MANUPIAN SECURITY official opened the door for me and I carried the tray with its jug of water and glasses through without a problem. I muttered a 'thank you' and I was in.

I was faced with an empty corridor consisting of four doors down the left-hand side. None of them had porthole windows like in the kitchen and all of them possibly had people behind them, which was a potential problem.

I listened at the first door. I heard nothing. I turned the handle and walked in.

Two women sitting at desks in a small office looked up.

"The meeting room's two doors down," snapped one of them.

"Sorry," I said and closed the door behind me.

Everyone was fooled by my catering uniform and my tray of props. It was amazing how stupid people could be.

I counted two doors down and stopped at the third door. Again, I listened. Again, I heard nothing.

Preparing myself for whatever lay beyond, I opened the door.

The room was unoccupied and lit by bright overheard lights. They shone down onto an elongated table which ran down the middle and was surround by six chairs – three placed on either side. The centrepiece was the tray of sandwiches the catering worker had carried up earlier. I placed my tray of water next to them and avoided the temptation to help myself to one of the sandwiches.

This had to be where James and Udinov would sit after their tour of the factory and discuss whatever private business they had. If I was to find out what they were up to, I needed to be a fly on the wall of the meeting.

But I was a very large excuse for a fly and the room had literally no hiding places. There was one table, six chairs and a blank display screen on the wall. I took out the P-tab from where I had stuffed it into my bra and brought up the recording mode. It would have to be my substitute digital fly.

I untied my ponytail and used the hairband to fasten the P-tab to the central leg of the table. I set the recording to trigger when the device registered sound. "Testing, testing. Hello, can you hear me?"

"I can hear you," said a voice.

I was so startled, I jumped up and whacked my head on the underside of the table.

There was no one else in the room with me. Puzzled for a moment, I rubbed my head. "Computer?"

"Yes," said the same voice. A female, unemotional voice. "What are your instructions?"

There were no speakers in the ceiling like in my ship. The computer's voice seemed to be coming from the blank screen on the wall. "Do you know what's going to be discussed at the meeting?" I asked.

"I have no information," said the voice.

The brief moment of excitement faded to disappointment. "Thank you, never mind," I said. Strictly speaking, using pleasantries when talking to a rudimentary machine was not necessary, but the line between artificial intelligence and dumb programming was blurred and I always tried to avoid pissing off a computer whenever possible.

"There is a presentation ready to be displayed," said the computer. "Would you like me to display it?"

"Yes please," I said, calculating how long I dare stay in that room before I was discovered. I probably should have already left.

"Presentation commencing."

The black of the display screen turned a dark blue and letters appeared in yellow: *Jonsonii Factory*.

"Turn up the sound," I instructed.

"This is a silent presentation," said the computer, as the letters faded away and video of the factory in operation filled the screen. The images were almost certainly recent as it looked no different to the factory floor I had just left, except the video was taken from a different angle from the one I was used to seeing from my workstation.

The image froze and statistics were superimposed on top:

*Factory workforce: 6,324*

*Support staff (catering, cleaning, payroll etc):157*

*Sick days: c. 15,000 / year*

… and so it went on. I drummed my fingers on the table. I really didn't have time to hang around for the presentation to get to the point, and without the script which was supposed to accompany the images, there was no guarantee it would ever get there.

I grabbed a sandwich and stuffed it in my mouth to quell my anxiety.

Salty protein paste squeezed through the bread with each bite while I rearranged the sandwiches on the tray to hide the gap I had created.

The screen changed into a schematic of the factory floor. The bird's-eye viewpoint marked out every workstation and every piece of machinery in a line drawing which showed how massive the factory was. A headline in red lettering – *Wasted Space* – appeared at the top. Red cross-hatchings drew themselves over the top of walkways and staff toilet blocks. The image changed to show the first floor with its canteen and offices, almost entirely crossed out in red.

So far, so uninteresting.

Until the images faded away and were replaced by a computer-generated vision of a new-look factory.

The shape of the old factory floor was still visible, but the workstations, the walkways and the toilet blocks were wiped out. In their place were machines. Vast, shiny machines everywhere linked by conveyer belts. The static image morphed into animation and the machines began to move as plain grey boxes of unidentified products were carried on the conveyer belts from one part of the factory to another.

Words in optimistic yellow scrolled over the top: *machines need no toilets, take no lunch breaks, don't get sick, work without sleep...*

As I read, muffled voices broke through my concentration. I pulled back from the table and listened. They were outside, there were several of them and they were getting closer.

"Computer: screen off," I ordered.

The screen went black.

I swallowed the remains of the sandwich and looked around. There was only one way out: back into the corridor where the voices were coming from.

Hoping my catering uniform disguise was enough to fool them, I opened the door and stepped through.

Outside, between me and the way to the stairs, were Grundor, President Udinov and Prince James. Behind them, a member of the Fertillan Guard – who I recognised from Prince James's ship – and a Manupian security official I had not met before.

The entourage took up the whole width of the corridor. They would have to step aside to let me pass, they would have to look at me and three of them knew what I looked like.

I turned away. There was one door left along that corridor and I needed to pretend that that's where I was going next.

"Looks like refreshments have just arrived," said Grundor behind me. At least my catering uniform had fooled him.

I walked slowly to the last door and reached out for the handle as I listened to the dignitaries filing into the meeting room. Their voices became muffled again as the door closed behind them. Inside, I knew the recording on my P-tab would have been triggered. As long as it wasn't discovered, it would be a simple matter to come back and retrieve it when all the security was gone, and I could discover the truth about their meeting.

But first I had to get out of there without being caught, and the Fertillan Guard and the Manupian security official – rather than go into the room with the others – had turned round to stand watch on either side of the door.

I had two choices: go into the last room in the corridor and face whatever was in there. If I was lucky it was an empty storeroom or something similar. If I was unlucky, I would have to explain what I was doing there to a bunch of office staff. Or risk walking right past the Fertillan Guard who knew me.

I decided the door was the best option, but when I tried to turn the door handle, it was locked. I had no choice.

My sweaty hand slipped from the handle and I turned back the way I had come. My beating heart urged me to run, but my calculating head forced me to keep an even pace. I looked straight ahead and kept my gaze directly on the prize of the door at the end of the corridor. Holding my breath, I passed the guards flanking the meeting room. Their eyes didn't falter from staring straight ahead. It was as if they looked straight through me.

I allowed myself a silent sigh as I passed.

I estimated I had five more steps before I reached the door.

*Five ... four ... three ...*

The door opened. A man in white catering uniform came through.

It was the same man I had soaked back in the kitchen. In his hands was a clean tray with a new jug of water and a fresh array of glasses. He stopped as soon as he saw me. His recognition was instant.

"*You!*" he shouted. "What the vac do you think you're doing?"

Behind me, I heard the click of guns being pulled from their holsters.

I swung my hands up under the tray and catapulted the whole lot into the air. Without waiting to see the man soaked with water again, I charged for the door. The security official on the other side

– who had so politely let me in minutes before – turned to block me, but he wasn't quick enough and I rammed into his shoulder to push him out of the way.

"Stop!" he ordered.

But I was running down the stairs, away from the sound of smashing glass and shouts of confusion.

An EE blast zoomed past my ear and struck the wall next to me. A warning shot. I kept running.

"Stop or die!"

I vaulted over the handrail as a second shot cut through the air where I'd been standing and seared into the wall. I landed, my knees bent to cushion the impact and my hands slapped on the floor to stop me falling forward. With the sound of chasing footsteps echoing in the stairway, fear pulled me to my feet and I crashed through the door into the factory floor.

The cacophony of machinery and people was suddenly loud and must have prevented anyone outside hearing the EE blasts on the stairs. Including the Fertillan Guard and Manupian security official who flanked the doorway I had just come through.

If they hadn't been there to stop people going through the door instead of coming out of it, I wouldn't have got away. But I was running before either of them realised what was going on. As I ran past her, I looked directly into the eyes of the woman in the Fertillan Guard uniform and saw that it was Louissi. She recognised me and I saw her eyes widen with astonishment before I dashed into the throng of workers and their machines.

The official who had fired at me on the stairs must have come through after me because the light of an EE blast sailed overhead. Screams erupted from the workers. One man stepped back from his machine as I was running behind him and knocked me sideways. I glanced back and saw the Manupian security official was at the door with his EEW drawn. Louissi and her Manupian counterpart pulled their weapons from their holsters. I kept running.

Down to the walkway on the far side of the building. Glancing behind, I saw the security official from the top of the stairs was only metres behind. He aimed the barrel of his gun right between my eyes. I cut sideways into another walkway and put workers between me and his line of sight. I hoped he wasn't stupid enough to fire and risk hitting them.

The exit was twenty metres ahead, but the Manupian security official from the door was coming round to cut me off. Louissi ran towards me from the other side. All three of them were armed, I had no weapon and I was wearing a crisp white catering uniform in a room full of people in drab clothing. The only thing that would make me more visible was a flashing light on my head.

On the wall ahead was the fire alarm. I swung my elbow into the protective cover and struck the button underneath. Sirens wailed all around. Workers groaned and looked for the source of the fire. The clanking, roaring and grinding of working machinery was steadily replaced by a mass of questioning voices as workers turned off their machines and asked each other if they really had to evacuate. In isolated pockets, they began to move back from their workstations, along the rows and towards the exit. Like sheep, others followed. Soon the whole factory floor was on the move. I lost sight of Louissi and the security officials as people came towards me. I ripped off my tunic – literally tearing off the buttons rather than take the time to undo them and dropped it to the floor where it was trampled by factory workers filing out.

I joined them, trying to hide myself among the masses, even though my dark-coloured crop top and white catering trousers didn't camouflage me as much as I would like. I nestled myself within a group of burly men all taller than me and shuffled along towards the one exit. If there had been a real fire, the volume of people, the single exit and the resulting panic would surely have killed hundreds, if not thousands.

No one else seemed bothered. They were just moaning.

"It can't be a drill," one of them was saying over the sound of the alarm. "Not with Udinov here, surely."

"I think the weapons fire must have set it off," said another.

"If some idiot's done it for a laugh, I'll strangle them with my bare hands."

I hunched my shoulders and bent my head forward as I tried to be inconspicuous among them. I reached out my hand to a workstation as I passed and grabbed a half-welded metal bar. I grasped it tight and held it against my thigh in case I needed it.

The lurching masses slowed even more as we got closer to the exit. A Manupian security official had somehow managed to get himself to the head of the queue and was working his way down, checking everyone. Very soon, he would be checking me. I gripped the metal bar tighter and tried to think of a way out that didn't involve surrendering myself.

He looked through the crowd and fixated on me. My gaze met his and we both saw, in that instant, that the game was up.

I switched back and bulldozed my way through the group of men behind me. They shouted protests as, head down, I ploughed through gaps between their bellies and elbowed my way through.

"Stop her!" cried a voice from behind. An EE blast ripped through the air above. Screams erupted and bodies surged as panic set in.

Two more gunshots zoomed over my head. People around me realised I was the target and staggered back out of my way, crushing complaining people behind them. It made getting through them easier, but also made me more visible to my pursuer.

I pushed through the last of the people to the back of the throng and into the clear space beyond. Turning to see the official still making his way through the mass of evacuees obeying the fire alarm, I knew I had vital seconds to escape.

At the back of the factory, crates of completed components were stacked into towers ready to be transported to their next destination. Somewhere behind them, there had to be another way out.

Weaving myself in and out of the crates, using the towers to shield my body, I came up against the back wall of the factory. Cut into it, at hip height, was a closed, airtight hatchway just big enough for a crate to get through. Or a crouching person.

I slammed my fist on the open/close button beside it and a warning siren struggled to be heard over the fire alarm. The door to the hatch began to rise slowly – too vacking slowly.

"Stop!"

I tensed. The Manupian security official was clear of the workers and his EE weapon was pointing straight at me.

"Turn round, slowly."

I obeyed. "I don't mean President Udinov any harm," I said.

"Don't care," said the official, pacing towards me, his gun ready to blow out my brain with a squeeze of the trigger.

I glanced to the hatchway to see the door had opened to reveal a conveyer belt which led into darkness. If only I could reach it.

"Hands up!"

I raised my hands slowly, my heart pounding so hard that I was shaking as I fought the urge to run. The metal bar was still in my hand; a useless weapon against the power of his EEW.

"Drop it!" ordered the official.

I lowered the metal bar and held it out as if I was about to let go.

At the last moment, I swung it round, struck the open/close button and jumped into the open hatchway.

He let off an EE blast. It streaked through the space where my head had been and struck the wall behind.

My bum landed on the conveyer belt and the door began to close.

He let off a second blast, but it hit the closing door.

I looked along the conveyer belt into what was a long, shallow drop into wherever the finished components of the factory ended up. The gap behind me was no longer big enough for a person to get through. I rammed the end of the bar into the mechanism, hoping it was enough to disable it and stop anyone following me, then I slid down the chute into the unknown blackness.

# CHAPTER FIFTEEN

I LANDED ON MY feet in darkness at the bottom of the shaft. Lights turned on above me, one after the other, in a cascade of brightness which illuminated a hangar with a ceiling as high as a house and filled with a row of transport vehicles. If the lights were triggered by motion sensors, it meant I was the only one there. It was likely anyone who had been in what appeared to be a loading bay had evacuated when the fire alarm went off.

I stepped forward and tripped over the corner of a crate that must have come down the chute before me. I stumbled myself upright and crunched on a thin film of yellowish grit like the natural dust of Manupia. I supposed the giant airlock on the other side of the transport vehicles led directly out onto the planet's surface where it was easy to take the crates to another factory to be assembled or to a spaceship to be taken off world. All of which explained why the hatchway on the factory floor was airtight: it protected the rest of the building when the airlock in the loading bay was open.

I tried the driver's door of the first transport vehicle, but it was locked. If one was locked, then I suspected they all were. Looking around for somewhere there might be keys, I saw evidence of the people who worked there. On one wall was a shiny whiteboard where someone had written what looked to be some kind of rota or shift pattern with a list of names, dates and times. Alongside it was a line of hooks with four breathers hanging from them. On the other side was a standard door which I suspected led into an administration centre and probably the rest of the factory. I tried the handle, but it was also locked.

I went back to the transport vehicles in the hope that someone had forgotten to lock one of them when they evacuated.

As I tried the third locked vehicle, the fire alarm suddenly ceased. To not have that incessant noise battering at my ears was a welcome relief. But, in the relative quiet, I heard the click of an opening door.

I froze.

"Sesaan Cassandra?" called a woman's voice from close by.

I shuddered at hearing my full name and knew instantly that it was Louissi from the Fertillan Guard.

"I know you're in here," she said.

I closed my eyes and leant back silently on the cool metal surface of the vehicle that refused to let me in. I was running out of chances.

"Give yourself up or I open the airlock and you can suffocate."

I took a deep breath of the oxygen-rich air around me. "You wouldn't do that," I called out, knowing my voice would confirm I was in there with her.

"Why not? If you die here, it will save me the trouble of taking you into custody. The Manupians will say you're an off-worlder who threatened the security of their president and Prince James will thank me for protecting the confidentiality of his mission."

I hesitated.

"I'm opening the airlock in three…"

She had to be bluffing.

"Two…"

Louissi was a dedicated guardswoman, but she was not a killer.

"One!"

Warning sirens wailed from above. She was actually doing it! In seconds the door would open and suck out all the air.

I ran down the side of the transport as I heard the hiss of the airlock release behind me.

I emerged into the open to see Louissi, wearing a breather, by the internal door. She swung her EEW towards me. I raised my hands.

The sirens kept wailing. I heard the rush of escaping air and felt a wind at my ankles as the outside sucked at the life-giving atmosphere on the inside and the gap between the opening door and the ground grew wider.

"Close the airlock!" I shouted.

The release button – a round, red knob underneath a safety housing which had been lifted clear – was on the wall beside her, next to the hooks with their three remaining sets of breathers.

"On your knees!" Louissi ordered.

I sensed the air thinning and my breath quickened to compensate. "Close the airlock!"

"*On your knees!*" The thin air barely carried the vibrations of her voice, but her meaning was clear.

I lowered onto my knees with my hands still raised and felt the last seconds of my life ticking away.

It was harder to breathe nearer to the ground where there was less oxygen and my gasps became more desperate as I struggled to get enough air into my lungs. I had a sudden memory of the Manupian woman who had attacked me on the surface and the fear in her face as she suffocated to death without a breather. Except, in my head, it wasn't her face that I saw fighting for life, it was my own.

"Pleas–" I didn't have the breath to finish even a word. "I surr–"

*I surrender*, I mouthed.

Louissi stabbed at the airlock control button with one hand while the other kept pointing the EEW at me. Wheezing through the pain in my chest and the pressure on my eardrums, the air gradually returned. I heard the final clang of the airlock close and the click of the seal shutting us off from the outside. I tried to breathe deeply, but my body took desperate, quick, shallow breaths as the dizziness from lack of oxygen subsided from my brain.

I looked up at Louissi. She had been wearing her breather the whole time. Her gun did not waver from its position trained at my heart. She was strong. I was weakened.

She pulled off her mask and reached down to the communicator on her lapel.

"What are you doing?" I asked.

She stopped before flicking the switch. "Calling for the Manupians to take you in."

"Don't," I said.

"If you're going to say you'll come quietly, then you should know I'm not stupid enough to believe you."

"You can't let the Manupians take custody of me. I'm on a mission from Prince Stephen."

"My loyalty is to Prince James."

"Then don't antagonise brotherly rivalry any more than they already have. Let me go."

"Don't be ridiculous!"

"Tell them I took a breather and went out onto the planet's surface."

"No!" Louissi flicked the switch on her communicator. "This is the Fertillan Guard in the loading bay. The suspect is here."

I flinched as I realised I was running out of time. I had to try something drastic. I lifted one knee off the ground and put my foot on the floor.

"*On your knees!*" she yelled.

"Why? Are you going to shoot me?"

I saw her waver for just a second and I knew I had a chance. I lifted the other knee.

"I will! I'll shoot you!"

"I'm in love with Prince Stephen. He loves me. You wouldn't destroy that, would you?"

I took a tentative step towards where the remaining breathers were hanging. She followed me with her EEW, but didn't fire.

I reached for the nearest breather and removed it from the hook. "Tell the Manupians I ran out onto the planet's surface. You can tell Prince James the truth if you like, but say it was to stop a scandal if I was arrested. Say you did it for Fertilla."

I reached out for the airlock release on the wall next to her and hit it hard to plant evidence for my cover story.

Sirens wailed again.

I put the breather mask over my face and tucked the air canister under my arm.

Louissi put her breather mask back on as her eyes stared out over the top of it.

I turned away from her and through the internal door which had to lead back into the main factory complex.

It was only when I stepped through and closed the door behind me that I knew for certain she was not going to kill me.

# CHAPTER SIXTEEN

MIGHT HAVE RUN directly into the path of the Manupian security officials if I hadn't heard them coming just as I was passing an unlocked door to a storeroom. I ducked inside and waited among the many shelves of cleaning supplies, with my ear pressed up against the door, until they had gone.

It was my first piece of luck.

The second was a cleaner's brown boiler suit hanging up on a hook at the back of the door. I disposed of my white catering trousers and climbed into them. The storeroom also gave me somewhere to leave the breather, which I hid behind a load of boxes at the back.

My third piece of luck was that it seemed Louissi had done what I had suggested and told the security officials I had escaped out onto the planet's surface. Because, by the time I got up to the main factory, through a door under the main stairwell I didn't even know was there, no one was looking for me inside. The last of the workers who had evacuated because of the fire alarm were returning to their workstations and restarting their machinery. As they were coming in, I was able to slip out without anyone giving me a second look.

After that, my luck ran out.

By the time I reached the transport station to take a ride out to the docking area, the place was crawling with black-uniformed Manupian security officials. It hadn't taken them long to conclude that I had either escaped across the planet's surface and had some-how got back into Shangi city, or hadn't got out onto the planet at all and was still in the city trying to get out.

I stayed there just long enough to watch people being stopped, one by one, and asked questions as they came and went from the station. All the security officials had P-tabs which they were show-ing to the passengers. I got close enough to hear one of them say my name – my real name – and I backed away. If they knew who I was, my picture was probably on their P-tabs and I needed to get out of there.

The only other way out of the city that I knew was an internal hub where supplies, such as food, were brought in from the outer docks and distributed in smaller vehicles to various places inside Shangi. Where vehicles came in, they could also get out. But that was also crawling with Manupian security officials checking each vehicle and drawing considerable complaints from the drivers caught up in it all.

I couldn't even send a message to Freddi. The P-tab he had given me was, for all I knew, still secured to the leg of the table in the meeting room in the Jonsonii factory.

I was trapped. The only other person I could turn to for help was Mel.

THE DARK BLUE door to number 185 was ajar.

My heart jumped as I thought for a moment that perhaps the security forces had reached Mel's flat before me. It wouldn't have taken much to piece together my name with the false ID I had used to work in the factory and trace it back to her.

But the door hadn't been bashed down. There was no sign of forced entry at all.

"Hello?"

I tentatively stepped inside.

The internal door to Mel's flat was also slightly open. From behind it came the faint sound of sobbing.

"Mel?"

I found her sitting on the floor of her lounge with a small, crumpled piece of paper in her lap.

Beside her, her father was slumped in the chair. His skin was so pale as to be translucent, his chest was still and his jaw had dropped open into a deathly grimace. The smell of coffee from a near-empty flask on the table beside him lingered in the room.

Mel looked up at me with moist, red eyes. "He's gone," she whispered.

"Oh Mel, I'm so sorry."

By the look of her father, he had been dead some hours.

"I think..." She gasped an emotional breath. "I think he did it on purpose."

"Don't be silly," I said. "He was an old man."

She held out the piece of paper. I took it from her.

In a rough, shaky, handwritten script, it said:

*You have no excuse now.*
*Go out and make a life for yourself.*
*Know that I always have, and always will, love you.*
*Dad.*

I handed it back to her. She snatched it away and held it close to her chest.

"Are you going to do what he wanted?" I asked.

"Leave Manupia? All I know is here."

"You have the means. You get other people off the planet. You could get yourself off."

She shook her head. "I don't know… another job… another place. The younger ones have the fight to start over. I don't know that I have."

"Mel, there's something I need to tell you about the factory."

She sniffed and wiped the tears from her eyes. "You found out what Prince James is doing here?"

"Not exactly, but I saw plans for the factory. I think they're planning to bring in automation. To replace most of the workers with machines."

"That can't be right," she said. "Manupia's strength is its work-force. Everybody knows that."

"Except the planet's being undercut by other producers out in the Rim using automated factories. If Manupia wants to compete and doesn't care about the workers, then automation makes some kind of twisted logic."

"We would all be workless. They wouldn't do that – they wouldn't!" A new stream of tears ran onto her cheeks.

"I saw the plans," I assured her.

"I thought you were here to spy on Prince James."

"The presentation I saw was meant for him, I'm sure of it."

"You're talking rubbish! Your planet is agricultural. Why show a prince from a food planet plans for an industrial factory?"

"I don't know," I admitted. "Perhaps Manupia needs investment from outside. I had to leave before I found out everything."

"You couldn't find *anything*," she said.

I sighed. I didn't have time to discuss it all with a grief-stricken woman. "Look, Mel, I don't know how long it'll be before they make the link between you and me. Grundor knows you brought me in on false ID, they could come here looking for me at any minute. I promise I'll get out and leave you alone if you want me to, but Shangi city is locked down. I can't get on a transport, I can't get to the docking area, I can't meet up with my crew."

"Why should I care?"

"I need your help to smuggle me out. I know you have a group of people getting off Manupia tonight. Make me part of that group. I can pay you. I don't have the money right now, but when I'm back on my ship, I swear I'll send it to you."

She looked at me blankly. I couldn't tell if she had understood me. I wasn't sure if she had even heard me.

"You could come too if you like," I said. "Honour your father's wishes."

She reached across and squeezed her dad's hand. She sat like that for what seemed to be many minutes as I anxiously waited for the security services to burst in and arrest me.

"Okay, Dad, I'll do what you want, you stubborn bastard." She stood and leant over to kiss him on the forehead. "I'll miss you."

Her final words to him cracked with emotion, but when she turned towards me, she seemed to find a new strength and the last of her tears fell from her face onto the floor.

"Are you ready?" I asked her.

She nodded. "Dad made me pack a bag for this day. I've always been ready."

# Chapter Seventeen

MEL TOOK ME to an abandoned factory on the opposite side of the city. The factory floor was half the size of Jonsonii, but its emptiness made it appear vast. Apart from a few remnants of metal frames welded to the floor, the workstations had been stripped out and what was left was cavernous nothingness. The lights which had once lit the space for thousands of workers had been turned off, removed or broken and so the only light came from the open doorway. It cast long shadows like tombstones as it hit the few metal struts sticking out of the floor.

Our footsteps echoed around the nothingness. They seemed to draw out other footsteps which shuffled in the dark. Faces appeared in the dim glow of the light. The faces of two women and one man. The younger woman I recognised instantly as Denni, the woman who had spoken to Mel after we left the factory the previous day, and the other two I didn't know.

"Mel, what's going on?" said Denni.

"We've been waiting," said the other woman.

"No one came," said the man.

Mel held up her hands to stop their questions. "There was some sort of security breech surrounding the visit of President Udinov and the Fertillan Prince which has snarled up all the transport in the city. There's been a delay, that's all."

"We're still going, aren't we?" asked the older woman.

"We have to," said Denni. "I've sold everything I had, made arrangements… I'm not going back to the factory."

Mel nodded, somewhat too vigorously to be entirely reassuring, and pulled her P-tab from her pocket. She had been exchanging messages constantly since we had left her home. She checked it again.

Denni looked across to me. "Hi, I'm Denni," she said, then introduced the woman as Vendra and the man as Kendov.

"Hello," I said, nodding at them all.

The others acknowledged me, but said nothing. They looked too nervous.

Denni, it seemed, was working out her nervousness by talking. "Are you coming too?"

"Yes," I said. "And Mel."

"Mel, really?" said Denni, excitedly. "I thought you said you had family ties keeping you on Manupia."

Mel looked up from her P-tab. "Things change."

Distant footsteps echoed from deep within the factory.

"Who's that?" I said. The footsteps were getting closer.

"Our ride," said Mel. "I hope."

Out from the darkness emerged a man. He was tall and broad, not like the native people of Manupia, and walked with a long stride that tapped on the solid floor with a firm, confident heel. As the light from the doorway fell on his face, it revealed only a pair of small green eyes set deep into their sockets. The rest was hidden under a scarf that covered his nose, mouth and chin, and by the hood of his top which he had pulled across his head and down over his forehead until it reached the ridge of his eyebrows.

"Which one of you is my contact?" he said, coming to a stop in front of us.

"That would be me." Mel stepped forward.

"You don't want to reconsider?" he said.

"Only if you don't want the money you were promised."

He chuckled and the material of his scarf fluttered with his breath. "I want my money as much as the next man, but I don't want to get involved in any local trouble."

"There's no trouble to get involved in," she said.

"What trouble?" said Vendra.

The hooded man turned to her. "I was stopped by local security before I got here – twice. They turn a blind eye to people cargo as a rule, but something's got them rattled."

"It was a factory visit by our president and a visiting dignitary," said Mel. "Increased precautions, nothing more than that. As I told you in the message. You must be willing to take us or you wouldn't be here."

I couldn't see his mouth under the scarf, but the way his eyes softened suggested he was smiling. "You must be willing to pay the extra or you wouldn't have come."

"You'll get it, I promise."

The hooded man grunted. "As long as you understand, you can't travel as passengers among the cargo like the others I've taken.

They're checking the transports for people. You'll need to travel as part of the cargo."

"What do you mean?" she said.

"I'll show you."

He turned on his firm heel and walked off the way he had come.

He called back: "Come on if you're coming."

We followed into the dark.

As we went deeper into the factory, the light from the doorway dissipated into virtually nothing. Up ahead, a beam of light suddenly cut a path through the factory. It made me catch my breath for a moment until I realised it came from a torch carried by the hooded man. It bobbed along as we followed him, never getting closer, never getting further away. As we walked, I heard the sound of things scuttling from the light.

"Do you think that's the workless?" said Kendov. "I heard some of them moved in here when the factory stopped production."

I shivered at the thought of people living in that desolate darkness for the rest of their lives.

The abandoned factory, although smaller than Jonsonii, had substantially the same layout and I recognised the route we were taking as leading to the loading bay. Which was confirmed when we stopped at the airlock.

"The seals on the exterior door to the loading bay have decayed over time," said the hooded man. "It's no longer airtight. We'll need breathers." He shone his torch along the wall beside us where four sets of breathers hung from hooks. He took the first one and strapped the belt with the air canister to his waist.

"There's six of us and only four breathers," said Mel.

"I think there's more inside," said the man. "Some of you will have to share until then."

"You *think*?" I said.

"If you're not happy with that, you're free to leave, but there's no refunds from here on in." He reached for another breather and handed it to Kendov. The final two were to be shared between Denni, Vendra, Mel and myself.

At least the power to this part of the factory was still in operation. The hooded man lifted the safety cover, pushed the button and warning sirens sounded around us. Moments later, the door began to open and I felt the draught of air move past my ankles as it escaped from the fully pressurised environment of the abandoned factory.

The rush of air wasn't as great as when Louissi had threatened to suffocate me back at the Jonsonii factory, which suggested it wasn't entirely exposed to the planet's atmosphere. I took a breath from the breather mask which was attached to the canister strapped to Mel's waist and handed it back to her to inhale before we stepped through.

Like the power to the door, the motion control lights still worked and blinked into life when it sensed our presence. They revealed a space almost identical to the one at Jonsonii except the layer of dust from the planet's surface was thicker and there was only one transport vehicle inside. It was the sort used for carrying cargo rather than people. At the front was a climate-controlled cab where the driver sat and in the back was a compartment for the cargo which was far from airtight. The thin membrane that covered the vehicle might have been enough to protect inanimate crates against winds and dust, but it was not strong enough to contain an atmosphere capable of supporting people.

Warning sirens sounded again as the door closed behind us. I wasn't the only member of our group to shudder at the noise. In a few moments, we would be shut in the loading bay and it would get a lot more airless.

I looked over to the wall where, at Jonsonii, they had kept the breathers. There was a row of hooks at this factory just the same with two breathers hanging from it. I breathed deep from the breather mask, gave it back to Mel and went over to the hooks. I put the mask on my face first, turned it on at the canister and breathed normally. The air tasted of nothing, as it should. I checked the canister which, fortunately was almost full, then strapped it to my waist. Once I was sorted, I took the other breather to Denni and Vendra.

The hooded man had opened the back doors of the transport to reveal it was stacked with crates, some of them as small as the ones into which I used to place my finished pieces of elbow-shaped metal components, but some much larger, about double the size. The hooded man was inside and shifting them about. He pushed one of the larger crates to the back of the transport and prised off the lid with a crowbar.

"You'll need to get in here," he said through the breather mask.

"*What?*" I said.

"You want to get past security?" he said. "You get in the crate. They're checking shipments of cargo, they're not checking the cargo itself."

"All of us in there?" Mel had to be thinking the same thing as me. There was barely room.

"Not all," said the hooded man. "I have two crates. Half of you can go in each."

Kendov jumped up into the transport and peered inside. "Just until we get into the spaceship, right? Not for the whole trip?"

"Right."

Kendov hesitated, like he was weighing it up in his head. He swung a leg over the side, stamped on the bottom of the crate like he was testing it for strength, then swung over the other leg. "Should only be a couple of hours, right? I can handle that."

Vendra looked warily at Kendov's crate. "We'll go in that one with you. Mel, you and your friend can go in the other one." Her words were determined, but her face was pale with anxiety.

Denni, however, hung back. "I didn't agree to be carried out in a box."

"It's the only way I'm going to take you," said the hooded man.

"I'd rather work in a factory all my life," she said.

"Are you sure?" I asked her. "What if they close the Jonsonii factory, like they closed this one?"

She shook her head in denial. The breather mask she wore did little to hide her terrified expression. "Mel's right. They wouldn't make someone like me workless. I'm going home."

She turned, ran for the door and slammed her palms against its closed, airtight surface. If she freaked out like that at the thought of getting in the crate, there was no way she was going to survive shut in it for a couple of hours. I walked over to the control and hit the button for her. She literally jumped at the wailing siren and kept shaking until the door had raised enough for her to get through, then she ducked under it and back into the main part of the factory.

I hoped she could find her way in the dark.

I pushed the control once more and the airlock closed behind her.

Vendra had already climbed into her crate and the hooded man had placed the lid on top which he was pounding to make sure it was firmly closed. He then prised off the lid of the second crate and stood before it.

"Ladies?" he said.

I looked to Mel. "Are you sure this is safe?"

"No," she said. "But it's the only way."

"You've used these people before? You can vouch for them?"

"I've used the network to reliably get up to fifty people off Manupia. Even dishonest people have an honest reputation to maintain."

She jumped up into the transport and climbed into the crate. I followed her, but not before picking up the crowbar from where the hooded man had dropped it. "I want to make sure I can get out again," I told him.

"Only when you're safely on board the ship and it has taken off. Come out before that and you risk getting all of us caught."

I nodded. I sat in the crate with my bottom in one corner and my legs stretched out across the middle. Mel sat with her bottom in the opposite corner and laid out her legs beside mine. The lid was put on top and we were plunged into darkness. My breath sounds quickened through the breather mask. Then several heavy blows thumped down from above, shaking the whole crate as the hooded man secured the lid on top of us.

I got a bad feeling that I had just done the most stupidest thing in my life.

I prayed to the Deity I didn't believe in and hoped I had not just been sealed inside my own coffin.

# CHAPTER EIGHTEEN

RIDING IN THE back of a transport across the hostile environ-ment of Manupia was the most frightening thing I had ever done. I had been in worse places in my life, but this was the first time I had ever trusted myself to a stranger. In other situations, I had always been able to talk or fight my way out of trouble. But shut in a box – relying on maybe only half an hour's air in the breather's canister, being knocked about and thrown against the sides as the transport bumped over the uneven planet surface – was something I just had to endure.

The cold from the planet leached in through the membrane of the transport and into our crate. Mel pulled out all the spare clothes from the bag she had brought with her and we huddled under them the best we could. The closeness of another human body was reassuring as I stopped being able to tell the difference between shivering with fear and shivering with cold.

We stopped.

"Are we there?" whispered Mel.

"Not sure." I listened.

In order for us to hear whatever was going on outside, the noise had to travel through the thin atmosphere of Manupia, into the membrane of the transport and past walls of the crate where we were incarcerated. It was an unlikely prospect. The more I tried to hear, the more I became aware of the pumping of my heart.

"I don't think I have much air left," said Mel. Her breathing was laboured. She should have at least another five minutes by my reckoning, but our fear had caused us to be greedy with our oxygen supply and we had probably both breathed too quickly and too deeply. She had also started using her breather before I put mine on, which meant if she had already begun to get low on oxygen, I was going to feel it soon.

"What's that?" said Mel.

I listened again. Quiet, but clear was the sound of sirens warning of an opening airlock. "We must be at the docking area. Hold on."

"I can't!" The thinning air was causing Mel to panic and the panic was causing her to fight for breath that wasn't there.

"Here, share mine." I cradled her head on my shoulder, took off my breathing mask and swapped it with hers. I let her take two long breaths, before returning it to my face. It calmed her a little as I acknowledged that it meant I had just halved my own air supply.

The sirens stopped and the floor under us jerked forward as the transport started up again. It almost certainly meant we were heading into a climate-controlled environment. Which meant breathable air and heat.

I think Manupian security searched our transport. I heard some-one climb aboard and I felt their footsteps vibrate through the floor as they walked among the crates and banged on the side of them. Mel and I looked at each other and said nothing. Vendra and Kendov must have also stayed silent because we weren't discovered. The crate remained sealed and the footsteps went away.

In the hours that followed, I imagined myself to be a polished, elbow-shaped metal component as our crate was thrown off the transport. We rattled around, hitting the sides and hitting each other as we were moved unceremoniously from unseen place to unseen place. At one point, Mel's breather canister flew up and hit her in the face. We had to stuff our mouths with clothes to stop ourselves screaming out.

From the jobs I had had moving freight, I knew we were being put onto a cart which trundled through the docking area where we were thrown off again, carried onto the spaceship and thrown down into the hold. The final jolt was that of the doors of the hold closing shut.

Then, nothing.

I waited as long as my impatience would let me, then I got to my feet and half hunched myself, half crouched, in the restricted space of the crate.

"What are you doing?" said Mel in an urgent whisper.

"Getting out."

"We're not supposed to until the ship takes off."

"It's fine. We're safe. I'm not staying in here any longer."

I put my back up hard against the lid of the crate and pushed. It didn't budge. I took a deep breath and tried to force my legs to straighten, but all it did was press my spine harder into the underside of the lid.

I reached for the crowbar and wedged it at the corner where the lid and the side of the crate met. There was no gap to lever it into, but I levered anyway. I kept pushing and prising the bar until it found purchase. I jammed the end into the tiny gap and twisted until the lid popped open.

The dim glow of the outside seemed bright after our incarceration.

I climbed out to see that the hooded man had been good to his word. We were in the cargo hold of a spaceship, much like my own, and it was full of crates, so although it was a large space, there was not much room to move around.

I helped Mel to climb out and we went round to the other crates, knocking on the sides of the larger ones until we got a response from Kendov and Vendra. I took the crowbar to their crate and got them out. Kendov had a large gash down his arm from where he had been injured in transit, but the blood had dried and he was otherwise fine. Vendra, like the rest of us, was a little bit shaken, but we had all made it through intact.

"This is the inside of a spaceship?" said Vendra, looking around at our unglamorous surroundings with childlike wonder.

"A not very impressive part," I said. "It's a cargo hold."

"The rest is more impressive?" she said.

"Not really."

I left them to recover from their journey and had a snoop around. It was pretty much a room with crates in it and the four of us. One wall consisted almost entirely of the airlock door which was used to bring freight in and out, while along the opposite wall was an internal door which led to the rest of the ship. I tried to open it, but it was securely locked. A third wall was just a plain wall, but behind the crates on the final side I found a full water dispenser, a collection of empty cups and a stack of three empty buckets.

I filled one of the cups and drank it down. The water was pure, cool and calming. I told myself I should sip it, but as soon as the water moistened my lips, I gulped it down. I re-filled my cup and took a second one back to Mel.

"Where did you get that?" said Vendra as she eyed Mel's cup jealously.

I handed her mine. "There's more behind the crates."

Vendra gulped it down like I had and I went back to collect another one for myself. Kendov followed me and I let him take his fill from the dispenser before me.

I looked again at the stack of buckets. "I wonder what they're for," I said.

"Latrines," said Kendov before gulping down his water.

I feared he was right. I had assumed that after we were free and clear of Manupia, we would be invited into the rest of the ship as passengers.

It was a foolish thought.

I imagined the money the others had paid Mel was well below the rate I would have charged for passengers. After Mel had taken her cut and passed on the fee to the hooded man who had passed it onto the spaceship owner and goodness knows how many other people in the chain, the price of transporting us must not have been much more than the price of transporting cargo.

That's what we were: cargo.

I returned to the others where I decided to keep my thoughts to myself.

Kendov and Mel arranged some of the smaller crates into a circle and we hopped up on them and sat facing each other, with our legs dangling off the sides, like we were sitting on purpose-made seats.

The ship stirred underneath us.

"What's that?" said Vendra.

"The engines," I said. "The ship will taxi out of the docking area to a designated part of the planet for take-off."

"Will it hurt?" said Vendra.

"No. There'll be some G-force, but it won't hurt."

Vendra, although not a great deal younger than I was, reminded me of myself when I first went into space. All wide-eyed and excited while, at the same time, frightened of the unknown.

I felt the rumble underneath as the ship propelled itself along. It was a comforting feeling. I knew all the procedures of lifting off into space from a planet's surface and we were following them exactly.

"Where are we going?" I asked. It dawned on me that it may have seemed foolish to wait until moments before take-off to ask such a fundamental question, but my plan was to get off as soon as possible after leaving Manupia to hook up with Freddi and I hadn't thought any further.

"To a new job and a new life," said Vendra.

"But what planet? What system?"

"We don't know," said Kendov.

Mel nodded. She seemed unfazed by the lack of knowledge.

"We go where the demand and the work is," she said. "People can move on from there if they want to. It's part of the deal."

I raised my eyebrows. It wasn't a part of any deal I would have signed up for.

"I was serious about the G-force," I said. "We should find a place to brace ourselves."

Jumping off the crate and feeling it shift position slightly underneath me, I realised that our biggest danger on take-off would be the crates shifting inside the hold. If we weren't careful, they could crush us to death under both their weight and the G-forces pressing upon them. So we pushed what we could to the back and sat in the narrow gap between them and wall which most likely lay towards the front of the ship.

The engine noise changed tone and the rumblings of power shook through all of us.

It was then that I realised Vendra had been staring at me for some time. "How do you know so much about space travel?" she said.

"I'm not from Manupia," I said.

She nodded. "I thought so."

"Then why are you smuggling yourself out with the rest of us?" said Kendov.

"It's a long story," I said as the engines roared around us, our backs were pressed into the crates behind us and the ship struggled against the planet's gravity to pull free into space.

# Chapter Nineteen

I TALKED THE OTHERS through each step of the journey as I recognised every change in engine sound and every shift in G-forces, like being back on my own ship. We pulled away from the gravity of Manupia and cruised through normal space to where I assumed we would reach uninhabited space and wormhole away. But I couldn't wait for that to happen. I needed to get out of there and signal to Freddi before we left the Manupian system.

I needed a plan.

As I was trying to think of one, the fatigue caught up with me and I fell asleep.

I was woken by the unlocking of the internal door. Dazed, I got to my feet as a masked figure entered. Like the man who had brought us in the transport, the person had a hood pulled down low over their forehead and a scarf which covered the lower part of their face. They also wore industrial brown-tinted goggles so even their eyes were hidden. The person was a lot smaller and slimmer than the man and, even through their baggy clothes, I could tell the body shape was that of a woman.

"Excuse me," I said, walking towards her. "I need to send a message to my ship to pick me up before we leave the Manupian system."

She turned to face me and that's when I saw the EE weapon in her hand. It was a small, personal handgun, but it was deadly enough and it was pointing right at me.

I held up my palms to show I was unarmed. "I don't want any trouble. I just need to contact my ship. Then I'll be on my way."

Her expressionless, goggle-eyes stared at me. I searched for the humanity beneath their brown tint, but there was none.

She chucked three small, dry bread rolls onto the floor with her other hand. They bounced away like children's playing balls. Backing away, with her gun still trained on me, she stepped through the door.

"No, wait!"

I ran to the door as the barrel of her EEW disappeared through it. The door closed and locks clicked into place.

I pulled at the handle, but it was unyielding.

"Hey! Come back!" I shouted, slamming my palms on the door. "I need to get off this ship now!"

I screamed out with frustration. I spun around and threw my back against its locked surface. I screwed my hands up into fists and banged them on the metal until the pain burned in my knuckles.

The others emerged from between the crates. Each picked up one of the rolls.

Mel wiped hers on her clothing – as if that was somehow cleaner than the floor – and offered it to me. "Want some?"

I shook my head. I needed to get out of there, not sit around eating dry bread.

"You should eat something." She broke the roll in half and offered me one of the pieces. "Take it. Space travel's making me feel a bit queasy anyway."

"Yeah, me too," said Vendra.

"I was thinking the same," said Kendov, clutching one hand to his stomach.

I took the roll from Mel and brought it closer to my face for an investigatory sniff. Something in the air turned my stomach. There was a putrid smell and it wasn't coming from the roll.

"Can you smell that?" I asked.

"Latrines," said Kendov.

As soon as he said it, I knew he was right. Someone had used one of the buckets for its intended purpose and we were sharing the air we were breathing with decaying human waste. I found something to cover the bucket and it helped quell the nausea, but only a little bit.

I retrieved the crowbar from where I had dropped it and went over to the inner door. I tried to wedge it between the door and its frame, but it was an airtight blast door and even the thinnest sliver of metal wasn't going to penetrate it. Not that I was going to let that stop me trying. Several times I managed to hook the flat end of the crowbar on the edge, but as soon as I put pressure on it, it pinged free. I tried and tried, beyond the point where I knew it was useless, then threw the crowbar right across the hold until it smashed into the bay doors with the dull ring of metal.

Eventually, Mel came up to stop me. She looked pale, like the bread roll had not agreed with her. "We should sit tight," she said.

"I can't sit tight."

"When they're ready, they'll let us out."

I shook my head at her stupidity. "How can you stand there and say that? You're putting your trust – your *life* – in the hands of strangers. You don't know their motives, you don't know their plans, you don't even know where they're taking you."

"I spent twenty years working for a factory, that's how. What difference does it make if we wander around the ship or if we sit here and wait patiently?"

"It makes a difference to me," I said.

Mel put out a hand to touch my upper arm in reassurance. Then she rested on it, to steady herself, as her other hand clutched at her stomach.

"Are you all right?" I asked.

"I feel a bit…" She turned and ran.

Moments later, I heard her throwing up behind the crates where the buckets were.

It was the first of many sounds of vomiting that I was subjected to over the following hours. All three of them were ill.

"It's being away from the factory," said Vendra.

"Don't talk rubbish," said Kendov.

"I heard that the workless fall sick when they lose their jobs," she continued. "Some of them even die."

"That's a rumour to keep you tied to the factory," said Kendov. "It's travel sickness, that's all."

I'd known first timers get travel sick, but not so violently and not everyone. Even I was feeling queasy and starting to get a headache. I wasn't sure if it was everyone being ill around me or the stress of the whole ordeal, but I definitely didn't feel well.

I *really* needed to get out of the cargo hold. If I couldn't open the door from the inside, then I was going to have to wait for someone to open the door from the outside. I just had to hope the woman who had brought the bread rolls would return. Because, when she did, I would be ready for her.

I retrieved my only weapon – the crowbar – from where I had chucked it and sat on the floor beside the door.

I waited.

My nausea got worse, not helped by the smell of sick which lingered in the cargo hold, even when we covered the buckets. I rested my head against the wall behind me and drifted off into a half-sleep.

It was the shift in the vibrations of the engines that woke me. We were coming to a full stop. Soon, the QED would fire and we would be wormholing to Deity-knows-where and my chance to send a message to Freddi would be lost. I gripped my crowbar hard. I desperately needed to fight my way out of there, but I could only do that if there was someone to fight.

The engine noise ceased completely.

"What's going on?" said Mel, emerging from between two stacks of crates. She still looked pale.

"Sounds like we'll be leaving the Manupian system soon and I'm going to be screwed," I said.

"Can't you message your friend when we get to where we're going?"

I snorted at the ignorance of people who'd lived their whole lives on one planet. "Messages can't travel interstellar distances. They have to be carried through wormholes by messenger ships and that costs money. If I was travelling as myself, then maybe I could find the resources, but I was working undercover and my fake identity has access to nothing."

The locks in the door clicked. I held up my hand for Mel to be quiet as I scrambled to my feet. I pressed my back against the wall and readied the crowbar to strike.

The door pushed open. I lifted the crowbar and swung it round as the goggle-eyed figure stepped through.

It struck her arm and she yelled. The lightning flash of an EE blast exploded from her gun. I was already ducking out of the way, but my reflexes were not fast enough and the beam of energy burnt into my elbow.

My scream echoed through the hold.

Searing pain cascaded up to my shoulder and down to my fingers.

Staggering, I fought through the agony and held onto the crowbar with sheer force of will. I swung back for a second attack, but the woman recovered and aimed her gun.

"Don't! Or I'll shoot you."

I stopped mid-swing. The barrel of her EEW was only centimetres from my chest.

"I'd rather get paid for transporting four of you, but I'll take a fee for three if I have to." Her words were muffled through the scarf across her face, but I didn't doubt that she meant it. "Drop your weapon."

I let go of the crowbar and it rang hollow as it dropped at my feet next to the drips of blood falling from my elbow.

My attack had done nothing, except maybe bruised her a little.

"Get back," she ordered.

Staring warily at her EEW, I did as I was told. Two, small, careful steps.

It was then that I saw Mel was standing behind the door. She had one of the buckets in her hand. She looked at me and, in that brief moment of unspoken communication, I knew I had to be ready.

The woman aimed her EEW around the room, but Mel remained unseen behind the door.

"I've come to tell you," the woman called out, "that we'll be going through the wormhole soon. You'll need to prepare to–"

Mel stepped out from behind the door and swung the bucket. A stream of vomit, urine and faeces flew out and struck the woman right in the face. She yelped in disgust and swung her EEW in the direction of the attack. But Mel had jumped out of the way and the woman – temporarily blinded by human waste clinging to her goggles – fired at nothing. An EE blast shot across the room and burnt a hole in one of the crates.

"Go!" cried Mel.

I was already running out of the door and into the corridor.

I didn't know the ship, but I knew small cargo vessels and this was no different to any other. I went up a level and found the control room.

It was compact with three seats and three consoles jammed into a triangular shape at what had to be the front of the ship. I didn't have time to figure out how to use any of them.

"Computer, close the door to this room!" I called up to the ceiling.

"I do not recognise that voice pattern," said an irritatingly smug voice from the speakers above. A male voice. Unusual and totally not helpful. "Please provide additional authorisation," it said.

"Drakh!"

I swung myself round to face one of the consoles. Without time to sit down, I tapped my fingers on the screen and brought up the controls for the room. I guessed correctly that this small cargo vessel had a similar layout and operating system to my own ship, so it was easy to find the control for the door.

Approaching footsteps clanged down the corridor outside.

I tapped the screen and the door slid shut. The locks clicked into place and I breathed deep. But it was the goggle-eyed woman's ship and it wouldn't take long for her to find out how to override it.

Gulping down my increasing nausea, I had to force my eyes to focus on the controls. A notification flashed up in the corner of the screen:

*Calculations Ready*

I tapped what I thought was the control to dismiss the notification, but instead I brought up the navigation panel with all the QED calculations. My finger went to swipe it away, but stopped as I read the destination:

*Leontes Station*

Keya's research station? That made no sense. There were no opportunities for factory workers there. It was a science station for scientists and support staff. It wasn't even anywhere near a transport hub which could take Mel and the others to a larger asteroid or planet where they could find work.

A loud banging on the door jolted me back to my more immediate problem. I swiped away the navigation panel and searched through for communications.

Locks clicked open. I had seconds before the woman came in.

I typed furiously as, without the help of the computer, I had to send a message manually: *Cassy to Freddi…*

The door swung open and the smell of sick and stale urine drifted inside.

The woman pointed her EEW at me as some of the contents of Mel's bucket still dripped from her clothes. She had, however, removed the scarf and goggles so I could see the face of the person beneath. I looked into her eyes and knew, immediately, that it was Patti.

"Hello, Cassy," she said, pulling back her hood to reveal her bleached blond hair beneath.

I felt queasy again and almost forgot why I was in the control room. I reached with my finger to send the message.

"Don't!" warned Patti, lifting her EEW so it was level with my eyes. "Freddi wouldn't like it if I shot you, but it doesn't mean I won't do if I need to. I could try wounding your other elbow. I'm told it can be quite painful if you do it right."

I clutched at my arm where the EE blast had burnt my skin and a wave of pain shot up to my shoulder and down to my fingers. The blood was sticky as I pulled my hand away. My stomach retched and dizziness made me stumble sideways.

"Not feeling well, Cassy?" said Patti.

"Everyone is sick. What have you done? Have you poisoned the air?"

"I'm breathing the same air as you. But the one thing I didn't do on Manupia was drink the coffee. Did you drink the coffee, Cassy?"

The coffee everyone craved at break time. The coffee even Mel's father needed when he was no longer working. Of course I drank the coffee. I was undercover. I had to fit in.

Patti must have seen the answer on my face. "Oh dear."

"What's it doing to me?" I said in panic.

"You're in withdrawal, Cassy."

"Withdrawal?"

"Did you not realise? Why do you think Manupia has a reputation for such loyal workers? You said working in the factory was fun – do you remember that? You were drugged, Cassy."

I felt doubly sick.

"Don't worry, you'll recover. They all do, mostly. It's why I make sure they stay in the cargo hold while they do it. They make such a mess."

"So this isn't your first time doing this?" I said. "You're a people smuggler."

She smiled. "Now you know."

"Does Freddi know?"

Her smile vanished and she waved her EEW at me again. "Step back from the console."

"I need to signal to Freddi. If he picks me up, I can get off this ship and out of your hair."

She pointed the EEW lower down my body. "I could shoot out your kneecap instead. I'm told that's even more painful than an elbow."

I stepped back from the console as a wave of nausea hit me. My stomach spasmed and I turned to throw up.

The remains of half a dry roll and yellow bile from my stomach leapt up my throat and spewed out over the floor.

I panted as I recovered and tried to spit out the vile taste in my mouth. Patti walked up behind me as I stayed bent over and readied myself to be sick again.

But I didn't get the chance.

Something struck the base of my skull and I collapsed to the floor. I stayed conscious long enough to realise Patti had hit me and then I blacked out.

# Chapter Twenty

I WOKE UP FLOATING in the gravity-free environment of an escape pod.

I reached out to the wall and, instead of feeling its solid steadiness, the action pushed me in the opposite direction and my back bumped against the other wall behind me.

The dizziness of drug withdrawal, being knocked unconscious and the effect of weightlessness sending more blood to my head than usual made me feel nauseous all over again. If I hadn't deposited most of my stomach contents in the control room of Patti's cargo ship, I might have actually been ill.

But I breathed deep, concentrated on the fact that I was alive and tried to focus.

The escape pod was probably designed to hold up to three people, but even on my own it was a small space. The bubble of human-sustaining environment had only three features: a hatch for getting in and out of, a cupboard in which there should be basic survival gear and a no-frills blanked-out control panel above my head.

I tapped on the panel and it came to life with a series of readings which seemed to make no sense. I steadied myself and focussed harder until I realised it was upside down. Or, rather, *I* was upside down in relation to it – there not being any actual up or down in space.

I spun my body around to the same orientation as the control panel and stared at the graphs. It estimated I had a little over two hours of breathable air left and power to run the heating and the other systems for at least three. The pod's fuel tanks were almost full, but that wouldn't get me very far. Escape pods are for emergencies and designed to sustain life until rescue, not for flying any great distance.

The distress beacon had been engaged, so at least there was that. Although it relied on someone being close enough to receive it and respond. Which they had to do within two hours if I was to survive.

I pulled open the cupboard and found it contained three bottles of water. I opened one and sipped. It was tepid, but my dry mouth welcomed it. I sipped again.

Also in the cupboard were some beige food cubes, the thought of which made me feel even more queasy, and some basic medical supplies. I took a dose of painkillers and hoped my stomach wouldn't throw them up again. Then I opened one of the cleansing wipes and did my best to clean up the wound on my elbow. As far as I could tell, it was only a flesh wound.

It had created a lot of blood and touching it with the cleansing fluid on the wipe stung like vac, but my elbow would heal.

Assuming the body it was part of didn't die first.

I considered my options. One: sit there and hope to be rescued. Two: do something to try to make sure I was rescued or, at the very least, die while fighting to stay alive.

Option two was the only option. I propelled myself back over to the console and considered my resources. The only thing I had was fuel. It wasn't enough to get me back to inhabited space, but it was enough to manoeuvre me a short distance. A moving target was a more visible target for potential rescue ships and so I fired up the engines.

Life erupted through my tiny vessel. Its power was pitiful compared to my ship, but it felt good to have its vibrations running through me. I set no course. Leaving the place where Patti had dumped me would take me further away from the area where other ships would be wormholing in and out, so instead I sent the little craft going round in a circle. Like I was marking my territory in that tiny piece of the galaxy.

A bloodied cleansing wipe floated past my eyes. In my semi-dazed state after becoming conscious, I must have dropped it forgetting I was in a weightless environment. I snatched it out of the air and stuffed it in the cupboard.

A wave of nausea overcame me and I leant my forehead on the cool surface of the cupboard door. I remembered my initiation at the factory and drinking down a whole pint of their coffee. They had me drugged up from that very moment. So when Mel's father had warned me not to get sucked in, it was already too late.

Static crackled out of the console. Its hiss spluttered into a voice.

"Cassy? Cassy are you there?"

I whipped my head round to the console. At the top of the display was a notification flashing from green to white telling me there was an incoming transmission.

"Cassy? This is Freddi. Respond!"

I hit reply. "Freddi? Freddi, where are you?"

"Cassy? Is that you in the escape pod?"

"Yes! Yes, that's me! It's so good to hear your voice, Freddi."

"It's good to hear you too."

"How did you get off Manupia? I thought the place was in lockdown."

"I let them search the ship until they were convinced you were not on board."

I was going to reply, but emotion was choking my throat.

"Standby," he said. "I'll come pick you up."

A droplet of water floated by my face. I was confused because I had been so careful when I had drunk from the water bottle not to spill any. Then I realised it wasn't from the bottle at all. The droplet of water was one of my own tears.

# Chapter Twenty One

THINK I MAY have hugged Freddi when he pulled me out of that transport pod.

The rest of it, I don't much remember. He put me into my room back on my ship and I slept for a long time. I got up at one point and went to the control room to take charge, but he simply led me back to my room again. I must have looked a mess.

We wormholed to Fertilla where Stephen saw to it that I received the best medical treatment. The medics patched up my elbow, checked me over, ran some tests and checked me over again.

No one asked any questions.

They let me rest.

Time became elusive. I'm not sure how long it was between the time I was rescued and when I was fully recovered and relaxing on Stephen's golden sofa in his ostentatious sitting room in Londos House waiting for him to come to discuss what we were going to do next. Freddi was there with me, wandering around the room looking at every single object he could lay his hands on, and some he couldn't.

"Sit down, Freddi," I urged him.

"Have you seen this place?" he said.

"Yes, I've been here before."

"It's amazing." He picked up a delicate ceramic vase from a shelf and turned it in his hand to reveal the whole hand-painted flower pattern which snaked around to the back. "What is this even for?"

"Put it down, Freddi. Stephen will be here in a moment."

"If he didn't want me to snoop around, he should have turned up to his own appointment on time."

He picked up a framed photograph from a table. "Is this King John?" he said.

The tall, proud man in the picture was dressed in fine clothes and standing outside on a planet with a breathable atmosphere. It was, indeed, King John, the nominal father of Stephen, James and King Richard. "That's him," I said.

Freddi peered at the photograph more closely. "Is that the one your mother was having an affair with?'

"Freddi!"

"What?"

"You can be so indelicate sometimes."

"Do you think he looks a bit fat?"

Mercifully, I didn't have to answer as the door opened and Stephen came in.

Freddi hurriedly put the picture back on the table where he'd found it and clasped his hands behind his back as if he had touched nothing.

Stephen smiled at us both. "I've ordered tea for everyone, if that's all right."

"Sounds good," I said.

"Or I can ask them to bring some coffee if you prefer," Stephen offered.

"Coffee sounds–" began Freddi.

"A bad idea" I interrupted. "Tea is good. We should *definitely* drink tea."

Stephen sat on the sofa next to me, and Freddi joined us on the other, identical sofa. Tea was brought on a tray by a member of household staff and was set down on the calf-height golden brown table between us.

I watched Freddi with amusement as he stared at all the ritual that went with having an afternoon drink at the royal household: the teapot, the cups and saucers, the teaspoons, the teaspoon rests and the pot of honey to add sweetness.

Then Freddi's amazement when Stephen did nothing with it. I knew it was brewing – allowing the flavour to seep from the dried leaves of the tea plant into the hot water in the pot – but I said nothing and let Freddi wonder.

"I've been looking at the export manifests for Fertilla over the past year," said Stephen.

"Fascinating," said Freddi, suggesting that it was quite the opposite.

"Actually, it was," said Stephen. "Especially with regard to exports to Manupia. There are an awful lot of them."

"That can't be particularly unusual," I said. "Manupia is a factory planet, it doesn't produce food, so it has to feed its workers somehow."

"I don't disagree," said Stephen. "But that fact alone makes it interesting for two reasons. Firstly, Fertilla must already have some sort of trade agreement with Manupia – whatever James was doing there, it's unlikely he was trying to sell them more food. More interestingly, the manifest also shows there is one farm almost entirely dedicated to growing produce for Manupia."

"That can't be right," said Freddi. "When I was running the farm, all our produce went into the common pool – well, apart from what we ate as a family and shared with the labourers. The system is designed that way so if one farm has a crop failure, the impact can be smoothed out by the supplies coming from other farms. Fertilla takes its share from the pool and the rest goes to export."

"Not this farm," said Stephen. "Tea?"

He picked up the teapot and poured a cup for each of us. As the golden liquid flowed from the white china, ribbons of steam twisted away until the vapour cooled and disappeared into the air.

Stephen took his tea plain. He picked up his cup using the saucer underneath and rested it on his lap as he sat back in the sofa. I added honey to my tea. The iridescent syrup slipped in a globule from the spoon and sank to the bottom of the cup. I stirred until it melted, then offered the pot to Freddi. He dug out a large spoonful which he dumped into the cup and stirred vigorously so the metal of the spoon chinked against the ceramic glaze inside.

"What's this farm got to do with automating the factories on Manupia?" I asked.

"Possibly nothing," said Stephen.

I sipped at my tea and hoped its sweetness could help join the dots in my brain.

"After all the trouble you went to, I can't believe that's all you found out, Cassy," said Freddi. "That the factories are going to be automated."

"All?" I said. "Thousands of people will be made workless. And that's just at the Jonsonii factory. Maybe millions if it's replicated across Manupia."

"Why would that involve Prince James?" asked Freddi.

"I don't know, but he went into a meeting room where a presentation was all set to go and explain how much more efficient everything will be if they replace people with machines. In theory, I recorded it all on the P-tab I left strapped to the table, but I can't see how we could go back to retrieve it now."

"Assuming someone else hasn't found it already," said Freddi.

"Indeed," said Stephen. "It's unfortunate because a recording might help to explain what all of this has to do with my brother."

"I'm sure I can find out another way," I said.

"You'll do no such thing." Stephen put down his tea to give me his full attention. "You've risked your life too much already."

"You're not kidding!" said Freddi.

"I didn't put myself through all that to give up now."

"You nearly got yourself killed, Cassy," said Stephen. "It's a warning sign and one you should take note of."

Freddi put his tea down hard on the table and some of it spilled into the saucer. "If you won't listen to your prince, listen to me. We've been through a lot together and that's the first time I've had to pull you out of an escape pod with less than two hours of air left. I say, let Stephen pay us, say thank you very much, Your Highness, fire up the QED and go to somewhere else in the Rim where we can take a safe, boring job."

"What about Patti?" I said.

I saw him flinch, even though he tried to hide his reaction. "What about her?"

"Don't you want to find out what she's up to?"

"She's a people smuggler, what else is there to know?"

"She was taking people to Keya's station where there are no jobs for factory workers. Why would she do that?"

"You don't know she was doing that. You were going through drug withdrawal, Cassy, and you were bleeding from an EE wound. You don't know what you saw on that display."

"I wasn't hallucinating, Freddi."

His stare became more intense. "What is it about Patti that you don't like? That she was sleeping with me? It's all right for you, you've got your prince lover waiting for you in your comfortable palace. What have I got?"

I kept my voice low and calm. "I don't have a problem with your relationship with Patti. What I have a problem with is locking people up in a cargo hold while they throw their guts up. What I have a problem with is people being made workless on Manupia so they feel they have to pay someone like Patti to take them away."

His face reddened with anger. "Patti was the one who put you in an escape pod and signalled me to pick you up. She needn't have done that. She may have been taking people off Manupia, but it was what they wanted and it was what they paid for. Don't pretend that you're somehow better than her, Cassy, because you've accepted some shitty jobs while I've been with you. I didn't judge you for it and you shouldn't judge her."

He stood up and headed for the door.

"Freddi–"

He turned to look at Stephen, ignoring me as if I wasn't there. "Thanks for the tea, Your Highness, but I'm going out into Londos to find somewhere that serves beer."

He pulled the door behind him. It was so thick and heavy that it swung until it was only half closed. It left a gap just large enough for me to watch him as he strode off down the corridor and disappeared from view.

# Chapter Twenty Two

Cocooned under the bedclothes, the warmth of Stephen's body mingled with my own. I felt safe. Contented. I felt loved.

I snuggled up closer to him and put my arm across his chest. I touched the first of his ribs on the opposite side and allowed my fingers to run down across each rib, like a vehicle traversing the bumps of an uneven road, until I found his slender waist.

"What are you doing, Cassy?" asked Stephen.

"Nothing," I said. The word was innocent, but my tone was entirely suggestive.

He picked up my hand and brought it back to his chest where he laid it flat across his breast, a lot further from his groin than I had intended.

"What are *you* doing, Stephen?"

"Thinking," he said.

"Ah." I turned back over and lay with my head flat on the pillow, looking up at the ceiling, just as he was doing. There was no point in trying to interest him in sex if his mind was elsewhere. "What are you thinking about?"

"My family."

"So they are more tempting than my naked body?" I said, sarcastically.

He propped himself up on one elbow, leant across me and kissed me on the lips. "Your naked body is always tempting, Cassy."

But the kiss was fleeting and perfunctory and before it had a chance to excite my desire, he had withdrawn it and he lay back on the pillow.

"What about your family?"

"Perhaps it's time you met them. Officially."

I laughed out loud. "I've already met your brother, remember? He dragged me into Londos House by the collar and called me a whore."

"All of my family," said Stephen. "If Richard and my mother can accept you, then James will have to come round."

"*King* Richard? You want me to meet *King* Richard?"

"And my mother. She's the key."

"I thought your mother was…" I tried to think of a polite way of saying it. The rumour on Fertilla was she'd lost her marbles not long after her husband, King John, had died. When her son, Richard, took to the throne she disappeared from view entirely and there was a second, more scurrilous rumour, that she had killed herself and the family had hushed it up.

"Her mind is not as sharp as it once was," admitted Stephen. "But she lives happily in her own rooms here at Londos House where she has her good days and bad days. A blessing on our relationship from her would do a lot to pull my brothers into line."

"That sounds…" It sounded very scary. "It sounds very formal, Stephen."

"We can't keep going on like this, Cassy. You going off and nearly getting yourself killed, then coming back for a session in bed with me, then flying off again."

"Maybe I like coming back for a session in bed with you." I pulled myself up to sitting and swung my leg over his body so I was straddling his hips.

"Cassy, what are you doing?" he said suspiciously, even though he knew exactly what I was doing.

"I'm bored of talking about your family." I leant forward, allowing my breasts to hang above his chest as I slid my hands onto the bedclothes either side of him. Then I lowered myself and brought my lips to his lips. I kissed him long and tender, allowing my tongue to wind inside his mouth to tease him before pulling away and savouring the taste of him.

"Are you trying to avoid the subject?" he said.

"I don't know what gave you that idea." I looked down at his groin where I could see his body was just as happy to avoid the subject as I was.

I ran my fingers down his side and this time I kept going beyond his slender waist until I touched the bone of his pelvis. I drifted over its contours to his stomach and the part of his body that wanted to be inside of me. I traced my fingertips until his penis grew longer and straighter. I smiled as it reminded me of one of his Fertillan Guards standing to attention. Except, this time, I was in command.

Stephen could resist no longer. He clasped my bum cheeks and pulled me closer. His body was as hungry for me as I was for him and he slipped easily inside of me. Our desire took over. Heat tingled as we pushed and pushed until every part of me was on fire.

Stephen sat up, grabbed my arms and suddenly we were rolling – entwined – across the bed until I felt the cool of fresh sheets under my back. He was on top where he worked to take me higher. My panting became sighing, became moaning, became shrieking as I burned brighter.

"Shh," he said gently. "People will hear."

It made me giggle. He giggled. But it was only a blip in our momentum.

At last, the exhilaration exploded and my insides were alight with a thousand supernovas firing in a scream of ecstasy.

Stephen reached across for a pillow and stuffed it in my face, but this only encouraged me to scream louder. I heard my own muffled cries as the final supernova burned bright and then subdued to a warm glow.

I reached for the pillow and flung it off my face.

Above me, Stephen was smiling and his body still had the glow of sex in the soft light of the bedchamber. "You were loud today," he said.

"Yes." I giggled.

He turned over and flopped back on the bed beside me; his head flat on the sheet where the pillow had once been. He started to giggle too. I don't know what was so funny, but we both laughed anyway.

I lifted the pillow from under my own head and scooted it across so we both could share.

As soon as he rested down on it, a heavy knocking on the door startled us.

I looked across at Stephen; annoyed that our intimate moment was being interrupted.

"Who is it?" he called out.

"Apologies, Sire," said a muffled male voice from behind the closed door. "Your vehicle is ready. You asked me to let you know when it arrived."

"Thank you!" he called out.

"Shall I arrange a driver?" said the voice.

"No, I can manage, thank you!" Stephen looked at me and sighed. "I'd forgotten about that."

"Going somewhere?" I said.

"I thought I could investigate the farm. Want to come? You should bring Freddi."

"Sure," I said. I stifled a giggle. "Do you think they heard us?"

He laughed. "I think they did. But I don't care."

Stephen called out from the driver's seat. "You can see the farm in the distance."

Freddi and I clambered up from the back of the vehicle and stood, clinging onto the back of Stephen's chair, to look out of the front window, as the vehicle rocked across the rough terrain.

The whole vista was unreal. Like the windscreen was a canvas and the landscape of Fertilla a painting laid upon it. The dusty, reddish yellow crust of the planet's surface took up more than half of the image until it met the line of the horizon where it seemed to fall into the soft pink of the sky. Standing proud of the line was the jewel of an agro-dome in a half-circle mound which glinted in the light of the Fertillan sun behind us.

"If you wanted to put a farm somewhere a long way from Londos city where people wouldn't accidentally stumble upon it, you would put it out here," Freddi observed.

The car's right front wheel struck an unexpected rock or boulder and the vehicle lurched to the left. My head banged on the roof.

"Ow!"

"Sorry," said Stephen.

"I could see why your staff suggested you get a proper driver," I said.

"My driving is fine," insisted Stephen. "I'm a bit out of practice, that's all."

I picked my way back through the car to my seat at the rear which had a seatbelt. I fastened myself in and told myself that the bumpy journey would soon be over.

Freddi joined me, but said nothing. I got the feeling he was still annoyed with me over what I had said about Patti. So I closed my eyes until Stephen's erratic driving brought us to the farm and we were able to drive inside onto the smooth surface of its garage.

We were greeted by the farmer, whose name was Pedri and was totally not what I had expected. Because Freddi used to be a farmer, my mind was expecting someone short and greying. Instead, a young, black-haired, skinny, tall man bowed before us as he recognised Stephen as one of the Regellan princes.

"Your Highness, Sire, I wasn't aware that you were coming." Pedri lifted his head up a little as he spoke, then bowed down again.

"Yes, I wanted to make an unannounced inspection."

"Inspection, Sire?" Pedri's eyes widened with shock.

"Inspection is perhaps the wrong word," said Stephen. "A look around would be a more appropriate term. I only didn't let you know ahead of time because I didn't want you to go to any trouble on my account."

"Yes, Sire," said Pedri. "Of course, Sire."

I was so used to behaving normally around Stephen that I forgot he was treated with reverence by most of the general population.

"Perhaps you could show us around," said Stephen.

"Of course, Sire. It would be my pleasure," said Pedri. "If you will excuse the mess."

I have been in many messy people's homes and Pedri's farmhouse was not one of them. Despite a pile of clean laundry stacked up on a table in his living room and some children's toys scattered in the corner, it was clean, generally tidy and obviously looked after. As we made our way towards the airtight hatchway that led into the agro-dome itself, a woman trying to settle a crying baby in her arms watched us from a doorway, along with two small boys, one of whom looked just about old enough to have started walking and stared at us curiously as he clung onto his mother's leg.

I braced myself for the experience of stepping out into the agro-dome. It was always breathtaking. I had done it maybe four times in my life and the sense of so much space around me was still unnerving.

Pedri, of course, took it in his stride as he released the seals of the hatch, waited for the hiss to equalise the pressure, and led us out onto his farm.

I tried to hide the sound of my gasp as my feet crunched onto Fertilla's dust and I breathed in the fresh smell of agriculture. Above me arched the translucent membrane of the dome which allowed sunlight in and stopped the atmosphere leaking out. Even though the sun was relatively low in the sky, I felt the warmth of its rays caress my cheek in a sensation that could never be matched by a fire or artificially generated heat from an environmental system.

In front of us were the branches of little trees about as tall as Freddi and adorned with leaves that seemed to create a green carpet as row upon row of the same species extended until they met the arch of the dome on the other side. The only noise was that of a harvesting machine working on the far side of the field and the sound of my own thumping heart.

I reached out for Stephen's hand.

"Are you okay?" he asked.

"I will be in a minute," I said. "I grew up in a city where I was never more than a few metres from a wall or the artificial sky and now I live in a spaceship. Agro-domes take a bit of getting used to."

Stephen squeezed my hand and I felt infinitely safer.

Pedri came up behind us. "Is there anything in particular you would like to see, Your Highness?"

"Why don't you show me around," said Freddi.

Pedri looked a bit put out, but Stephen nodded his approval to the plan and the two farmers – well, one current farmer and one former farmer – left us to stare out at the field.

"That's a lot of trees," said Stephen.

"Yes," I said.

We continued to look out at the breathtaking sight as I sensed Stephen was building to say something.

"Did you think about what I said this morning?" he asked, eventually.

"About meeting your family?" I said. "I don't know if I'm ready for that."

"My mother's a bit absent-minded, but she's not a monster."

"It's not meeting her that bothers me. I don't mind meeting your mother, or King Richard for that matter, it's what the meeting represents. Making our relationship formal, like it's part of some kind of royal protocol."

"We can't go on as we are forever."

"I know." He was right, for vac's sake. How dare he be right? I didn't want to choose between a life in space and a life in the palace. I wanted it all.

"When my father was alive, he told me a man in my position would never have to worry about finding a woman to be with. He said all women dream of being with a prince."

"But that's all it is, isn't it? A dream," I said. "They dream of being a princess, having fine clothes and doing whatever they want because they'll never have to worry about money ever again. But marrying into royalty is entering a gilded cage, isn't it? You can't do what you want because there are certain expectations and duties you have to fulfil."

"It isn't as bad as that," said Stephen.

"You're the head of the Fertillan Guard. Is that really what you wanted to do when you grew up?"

He shrugged. "It's what I was assigned to do. What I wanted didn't come into it."

"Exactly."

He looked crestfallen.

"All I'm saying is, I fell in love with *you*, not your job. I want to be with the man, not the prince."

"And I want to be with you, Cassy."

I blushed a little bit and, to hide my embarrassment, let my hand slip from his fingers and stepped out into the line of trees. "What do you think these are?" I said, in a blatant change of subject.

"Trees," he said.

"Obviously they're trees! What sort of trees?" I touched one of the leaves and rubbed it between my thumb and forefinger. It felt waxy.

"I thought they might be fruit trees," said Stephen. "But Fertilla hardly produces any fruit. It takes too much sun and water."

I reached in among the leaves again and pulled off some of the berry-like fruits from one of the branches. Most of them were red, but some were green, while others were half green and half red. "What are these?"

Stephen shrugged. "I suppose they must be tree fruit, but it's not like any fruit I've ever seen."

"You've seen a lot of fruit, have you?" Fruit was considered so much of a luxury, it was regarded as almost a myth in some parts of the Rim.

"It's one of the advantages of living in a gilded cage," he said.

I heard footsteps and saw Freddi was approaching from alongside the line of trees. Behind him, Pedri had turned to go back into the farmhouse.

"Well, that was interesting," said Freddi when he reached us.

"Did you find out what they grow here?" said Stephen.

Freddi stood sideways and held out his arm to indicate the vast plantation in front of us. "I thought that was obvious."

"Trees," said Stephen.

"That have these little things growing on them." I held out my palm to show him the red and green berry-fruits I'd picked.

Freddi looked from me to Stephen and then back to me again. "You don't know what they are, do you?"

We were both too embarrassed to answer.

Freddi shook his head. "I don't believe both of you grew up on a farming planet and you don't know barely anything about farming. Look–"

He took one of the red berries from my hand and pressed his thumbnail into the flesh. He peeled it to reveal a greenish white pip or stone inside. "You know what this is now?" he asked.

Stephen peered at the stone. "Let's pretend that we don't."

"It's a coffee bean," said Freddi.

I looked at it again. "But coffee is black."

"*Roasted* coffee that they make the drink from is black. Raw coffee looks like this."

"This whole farm is growing coffee?" said Stephen.

"More or less," said Freddi. "Which makes sense, if you think about it. People on Manupia drink a lot of coffee and it has to come from somewhere."

"Is it possible my brother did a deal to grow coffee especially for Manupia?"

"Probable, I'd say," concluded Freddi. "Pedri is a big fan of Prince James. He's been telling me how Prince James looks after his family, how he makes sure his farm gets all the help it needs. He talks about Prince James almost every sentence."

I took the raw coffee bean from Freddi's hand. "Then this is special drugged coffee?"

Freddi shook his head. "No, I don't think so. Pedri says his family dry and roast a little of the stuff to drink themselves. There's also a small shipment that gets sent to the Fertillan produce pool after every harvest. I think this is regular coffee."

"But the coffee I drank was drugged," I said.

"Which brings me to the other thing they grow here." Freddi reached into his pocket and pulled out a bunch of leaves which had already started to wilt from being picked from the plant. "Pedri grows this in a small field round the back. He calls it po-go weed. He told me, it's a herb considered to be a delicacy in one part of the Obsidian Rim and yields him a good price, which is why he grows it. Except, he tried putting some in the family meal one night and it added no flavour to the stew whatsoever. In fact, he seemed to think it made them all a bit ill. Which makes me suspect–"

"–that po-go weed is what the Manupians are putting in the coffee they give to the workers," I said.

"Precisely," said Freddi. "A tasteless narcotic, just the sort of thing you need if you want to feed drugs to someone without them knowing."

"Which suggests," said Stephen, "that my brother is fully aware that the Manupian workers are kept loyal with drugs fed to them by their factory bosses."

"I would say so, yes," said Freddi.

"So what happens if the Manupian factories become automated?" I asked. "Who's Pedri going to sell his coffee to then?"

At that point, Pedri came out of the farmhouse and waved across to us. "Your Highness, would you like some our home-made soup? My wife makes it, it's very good."

Stephen looked across at Freddi, who nodded that it was

probably a good idea. "Yes, thank you," Stephen called and headed back inside.

Freddi and I followed.

"I can't believe this whole thing is to do with the trade in coffee," I said to Freddi. "There has to be more to it."

"I hate to agree with you, Cassy, but I think you're right."

"So, what do we do now? We've run out of leads."

"I'd like to go to Leontes, if you can spare the qubition, Captain. I have unfinished business with Patti."

"I thought you said I was hallucinating when I saw that destination on her ship."

"Well, like you said, we've run out of other leads."

"Okay, Leontes it is."

# Chapter Twenty Three

Leontes Station let us dock, even though we weren't expected, and we disembarked into the hangar where we had, not so long ago, unloaded and loaded two lots of cargo. It was even quieter than our last visit, with no cargo at all cluttering up the space, just a couple of other docked ships and a confused-looking woman in overalls who came up to us while looking at something on her P-tab.

"You deal with her," Freddi said in my ear. "I'm going to have a look around."

He peeled off to one side as the woman stopped in front of me and gave me a friendly, if bemused, smile. "I don't seem to have you listed," she said.

"No, we were just passing and thought we might drop in to see Keya," I said.

"Just passing? *Leontes?*"

There were a few other inhabited stations orbiting the sun's only gas giant in the Leontes system, but none of them were anything other than small civilian colonies, as far as I knew. There had to be a reason for anyone to travel there and that would involve wormhole travel unless the traveller was prepared to spend the many years it would take to get there through normal space.

"When I say 'just passing', I more sort of meant we were at a bit of a loose end and thought we might pay her a visit."

"Keya…?" said the woman, consulting her P-tab.

"Doctor Keya Sharma," I elaborated.

"Hey, Cassy!" Freddi called out. "You need to see this."

He was standing by one of the other ships docked in the hangar. I walked over as the woman in overalls tried to contact Keya.

"This is Patti's ship," said Freddi.

I looked up at the cargo vessel which, although small, looked large in the confined space. It was typical of its type with a front section which narrowed into a cone and a rear with large cargo bay doors. It was old, somewhat battered with carbon scars from many landings and take-offs from planets with atmosphere. It was certainly like Patti's ship, but the Rim was full of vessels like that.

"Are you sure?" I said.

"Definitely." He touched the side of it and the carbon deposit blackened his hand.

"But Patti would surely have left by now. We didn't exactly rush after her."

"I'm as surprised as you, Cassy. I thought we would find out what she was doing here and what she did with your Manupian factory friends, I didn't expect her to actually be here."

"And yet," said a female voice behind us, "here I am."

We spun round to see Patti, her hair as bleached blond as ever, walking towards us and pushing an upright trolley with three identical boxes stacked up on it. She brought the trolley to a halt and let it rest on its base as she stopped in front of us. I don't know which of the three of us was more surprised and we stood staring at each other for some time before any of us spoke.

"I see Freddi rescued you from that escape pod, Cassy," said Patti eventually.

"Am I supposed to thank you?" I said.

Patti smiled. "Thanks would be nice, but it's not necessary."

"What are you doing here, Patti?" Freddi's tone was accusatory and stripped of whatever emotion was lying underneath.

"It's good to see you too, Freddi."

"That doesn't answer my question," he retorted.

Patti reached into her pocket and pulled out a small remote control like the one we had for our own ship. The metal of the cargo bay doors groaned and released its locks as the doors opened to reveal the hold that I had come to know too well during my incarceration. It had the faint odour of disinfectant from where it had been cleaned of vomit.

Patti picked up the top box from the stack she had wheeled over. "I'm taking medical supplies back to Manupia," she said as she passed us and went inside her ship.

I think she must have seen my disbelieving expression because she came back out again and stopped in front of me, giving me a superior look. "What? Don't think I'm capable of being a humanitarian? Just because I used to be a pirate, Cassy, doesn't mean I'm without morals."

She strode right past me and picked up the second box.

"Look," she said, and turned it round so I could see the universally acknowledged red crescent symbol of medical supplies. She held out her hand to Freddi. "Can I borrow your knife?"

Freddi reached inside his jacket and pulled out the fifteen-centimetre blade that he kept there. I suspected Patti had a knife of her own hidden about her person, but she asked Freddi for his to show she had intimate knowledge of him.

She took the knife, cut through the box's packing tape, opened the flaps and revealed around two dozen sealed medical vials with the code 'P1-N5' written on a white sticker on top of each of them.

"See?" She handed Freddi's knife back to him. "Medical supplies. I had to wait for them to be ready, which is why I'm still here. Otherwise, as you say, I would have been long gone by now."

"What about the factory workers from Manupia?" I said.

"The ones who threw up all over my cargo hold?" said Patti. "Delivered safely to this very station."

"What does a science station want with three factory workers?" I said.

"You should ask them," said Patti. "Cheap labour, I should imagine. A science station isn't only full of scientists, you know. They need people to clean and cook and maintain the place – just ask this person here."

Patti pointed to the woman in overalls who had been standing at a discreet distance and watching everything with increasing confusion. "Me?" she said. "Ask me what?"

Patti folded back the flaps of the box and took it to join the other one in the cargo hold. I watched her load the third and final box, not knowing what to say. I was angry at her for locking me up in her ship, I was angry at her for shooting me in the elbow and

I was angry at her for leaving me unconscious and drifting in the escape pod. But none of what she did, on the face of it, seemed unreasonable.

Having collected her trolley, Patti wheeled it towards Freddi. She whispered to him, like it was a private conversion between the two of them, but spoke loudly enough so I could hear. "If you ever want to crew with me, Freddi, you know you only have to ask."

"Patti…" I could see that he was tempted.

She turned to me. "He's very loyal to you, Cassy. You have no idea. I don't understand what you see in your prince. You have all the riches you need on your ship already."

Patti leant forward and planted a kiss on Freddi's lips. She put her hand around the back of his neck and drew him closer. Freddi stood there and allowed her embrace, but didn't kiss her back. Like he was embarrassed to in front of me.

Eventually she pulled away from him and left him staring, not able to bring himself to say anything.

"So very loyal," said Patti with a self-satisfied grin and wheeled her trolley away.

Keya came down to the hangar looking immaculate, as she always did, in her scientist whites. She hugged me and then she hugged Freddi, but she did so with less enthusiasm than I remembered from when we had arrived with cargo.

"Are you okay?" I asked her. Even through her expertly applied make-up she looked tired.

"I should be on rest cycle," she said. "But I've been working in the lab to finalise proposals for a new project after my last one was taken away." She shook her head as if to shake herself free of her work problems. "Anyway, what are you doing here? I thought you had gone back to Fertilla."

"We're looking for three factory workers," said Freddi. "They came here on board that ship over there." He pointed towards Patti's vessel, still sitting in the hangar with its cargo bay doors wide open.

"Factory workers? On Leontes?" said Keya. "What use would we have for them?"

"They were under the impression they would find jobs here," I said. "Not science jobs, obviously. Manual labour, that sort of thing."

"I don't think so," said Keya. "All ancillary workers are vetted before they arrive and chosen to do a specific job. I can't imagine factory workers would fit into that category. At least, they certainly wouldn't when I was running Octavia Research Station. I'm just an employee here, of course."

She called over the woman in overalls and got her to look up the arrival and departure logs for the station. She easily found the entry for Patti's ship which stated that three passengers – two women and a man – had arrived five days before.

The woman showed Keya the readout on her P-tab. Keya snatched it out of her hand and peered closer. She scrolled through the entry and seemed to read it over several times as her face went ashen.

"What is it?" I said.

"They were assigned to Section Five."

"What's Section Five?" I said.

"The isolation lab."

KEYA RAN THROUGH the station, so fast that Freddi and I only caught up with her as she stopped to pass the identity checks at each security door which separated the complex into different areas.

"Keya, what's so significant about the isolation lab?" I called after her.

She kept running.

We passed a couple of other people in scientist whites who pressed themselves against the walls of the corridor to make way for us as we scooted past.

She paused at another one of the security doors and pressed her hand against the reader by the side. A light scanned her palm and the locks of the door clicked open.

"Keya!" said Freddi. "Will you stop and talk to us?"

She didn't answer. The door slid open and she was running again. I chased after her with Freddi struggling to keep up due to his bad hip.

I paused as we reached a sign to Section Four and looked back, but Freddi signalled me to keep going.

I ran faster and caught up with Keya as she turned a corner to where a security door marked the entry point to, according to the sign above, Section Five.

I slipped past Keya and stood in front of the reader so she couldn't access it.

"Out of the way, Cassy," she said, breathing deeply from running.

"Not until you tell me what's going on."

She hesitated.

Freddi came limping around the corner and, seeing us both standing there, slowed to a walk and leant against the wall to catch his breath.

Keya swallowed hard. "My project was taken away from me suddenly and unexpectedly some months ago."

"Was that the vaccine for the plague?" I said.

She nodded. "That's right, I forgot I told you. We had a breakthrough, I thought. The antibodies destroyed the virus in the lab, we were ready to go to trials and then… Cassy, please get out of the way, I've got to get in there. If only to prove I'm wrong."

"Wrong about what?" said Freddi.

But Keya didn't answer, she pushed me out of the way and slammed her palm down on the reader. "Please say I have security clearance for this section," she whispered to herself. The light scanned beneath her fingers. "Come on, come on, come on!"

Locks clicked and the door slid open.

Inside was another corridor, but in darkness.

"Where is everyone?" said Freddi.

"It's rest cycle," said Keya. "They're sleeping or eating or having sex, I imagine."

She stepped inside and the motion-sensor lights in the ceiling blinked their illumination down upon her.

The corridor was narrow with two manually operated doors set into each side and a fifth door at the end labelled 'Observation'. Keya headed straight towards it.

Lights turned on as she stepped inside the observation room. But, there, she stopped.

"By the Deity," she said under her breath.

"What?" I said.

"Guinea pigs," she said. "Guinea pigs."

I pushed past her. But when I got into the room, I also stopped.

It was small, only just big enough for the three of us to fit in there. Down one side was a desk with three computer screens set in it and above – dominating the room – was an internal window looking into a much bigger room on the other side. The room being observed had three narrow beds pushed up against each of the other walls. The ones on the side walls appeared to be occupied by people with the covers pulled over them, but the one straight out in front of us was not. Beside it, on the floor, sat a woman with her knees up to her chest and her arms and head resting on them so the top of her head was facing towards us.

"Are they your factory workers?" asked Freddi.

I couldn't tell. I reached over the desk and knocked on the window. "Mel? Mel?"

None of them moved.

"They can't hear you," said Keya as she pulled herself away from the doorframe and stepped all the way into the room. All the colour had drained from her face and not even the pigment of her make-up could disguise it. "It's a sealed room."

"What are they doing in there?" I said. "Can I speak to them?"

Keya nodded. She tapped one of the screens and it lit up with a panel of controls which were headed, 'Isolation Room'. She touched one of them and the sound of a man coughing broke through speakers embedded in the desk. Through the glass, I saw the person in the bed on the left convulse with each cough.

Her hand shaking, Keya hovered her index finger over a control which said 'Intercom'. "Touch this to speak to them. Take your hand away and it cuts out."

I hit the control with more force than necessary. "Mel? *Mel?*" I yelled at the window.

The seated woman lifted her head and I saw that it was her. She looked about the room nervously. "Hello?"

A woman's retching cough almost drowned out her voice as the figure in the bed on the right convulsed.

"Mel, it's Cassy. Are you all right?"

"Cassy? Where are you?"

"Behind the glass."

Mel got to her feet and came right up to the window. She put her hands against the glass and pressed so hard that the underside of her palms flattened and paled against the surface.

"You need to get us out of here! Vendra and Kendov are really sick. They need medical help."

"I'm coming, Mel, hold on!"

But Keya pulled my finger away from the intercom and cut off my communication to Mel. "You can't get them out, they're in isolation."

"But they need help."

As if to prove the point, both Vendra and Kendov broke into an ugly lung-wrenching coughing fit.

"Keya," said Freddi. "What are guinea pigs?"

She swallowed hard and leant back against the wall behind her like the question took away her strength to stand. "They are small rodents from the time before the Oblivion War. They were used in scientific tests."

"I don't understand," I said.

A tear fell from Keya's eye and she wiped it away from her cheek. "They wanted to proceed straight to human trials, and I said no, it's not safe. What works in a test tube in a lab, doesn't always work in the real world, you know?" Her voice cracked with emotion. "They said, 'oh but, Keya, the client needs the vaccine now' and I said it wasn't ready. So they took the project away from me. They said they were sending it to a bigger lab with better computer modelling, more staff – and I stupidly believed them."

Freddi grasped both of Keya's hands and gently pulled them towards him so she lifted her head. He looked directly into her eyes. "Are you saying someone deliberately exposed these people to the plague?"

She nodded and more tears fell. "They must have been doing it all these months."

Mel banged on the window with her palm. "Hey! What's going on?"

I touched the intercom control. "Hold on a minute, Mel, we're just…" My mind fumbled for an excuse. "Looking for the key."

"If that's the plague," said Freddi. "Why are only two of them sick?"

Keya looked across to me. "Ask your friend what happened. Why they are in there."

I did as she asked.

"We're in quarantine," said Mel. "They gave us some inoculations against diseases we don't have on Manupia. It was after that, I noticed Vendra and Kendov started coughing. I thought it was effects of leaving the factory, but they're so much worse. How much longer, Cassy?"

Keya wiped her eyes on the sleeve of her white tunic and smeared the black of her eye make-up over it. She brought another one of the screens to life, and nodded as she read something that made her cry all over again.

"Your friends were each given an injection in a blind trial," she said. "One received the vaccine and two were given a placebo. Then they were put into isolation and exposed to the plague. I would say that your friend Mel was the one who received the vaccine."

"If the other two have the plague," said Freddi, "then they're as good as dead."

"We have to get Mel out of there." I headed for the door.

"Wait!" said Keya. "You can't just let her out, she'll be contaminated. You'll expose the whole station to the plague. You two might be immune, but I'm not and neither is anyone else on this station."

"You can't leave her in there!" I looked through the glass to see Mel had walked away from the window and was now pacing the room.

"We can use decontamination procedures," said Keya. "The same way you did when Doctor Raymon died aboard your ship. The isolation room is designed to put people in and out of quarantine. It should be relatively straight forward."

I pressed the intercom. "Hang on, Mel. We're coming."

"Are you going to tell her we can't save the other two?" said Freddi.

"Not until we have to," I said.

# Chapter Twenty Four

OUR FIRST PRIORITY was getting Mel out of the isolation room and then deciding how we were going to tend to Kendov and Vendra. Mel would have to pass through a series of compartments which required her to strip out of her clothes, take a decontamination shower and finally emerge cleansed of any traces of the virus.

But, as the room was locked from the outside, it required one of us to go in and get her.

"I'll go," I said.

Keya looked me up and down in my regular shirt, jacket and trousers. "Not like that you're not."

"You've already tested me and know I'm immune to the plague."

"No reason to take any chances. You'll need to wear a biohaz-ard suit." She looked around, but the only thing in the annexe to the isolation room was the entrance to the room itself via a door marked 'Decontamination Chamber'.

"There'll be some in Section Five. No one works with deadly viruses without one to hand."

"Then we'll go find one," said Freddi.

There were three unexplored doors in Section Five and three of us, so we took a room each.

I was the one who picked the right room. It was some sort of storeroom entirely full of scientific equipment, most of which I'd never seen before, but just inside the door was a rack with three yellow, evi-plastic biohazard suits hanging from it.

"Got one!" I called out and pulled one down from its hanger.

A woman's scream rang out down the corridor.

"Keya?"

I dropped the suit and ran out of the room.

"No, no, no!"

I followed the sound of her voice into an open door where she stood with her hands clasped to her face and stared out at a room full of refrigerators.

Freddi came in moments after me. He looked around at the seemingly innocuous array of glass-fronted cooling cabinets, many with vials of labelled scientific samples. Other than a bench with a couple of computer screens embedded in it, the room contained nothing else.

"What happened?" said Freddi.

"That fridge should be full," said Keya. She pointed a shaky finger at the glass-fronted cabinet next to her. While the other fridges were largely stacked with vials, the shelves in that one were empty. "This is the secure section where we keep all the controlled samples. I requisitioned samples from here when I was developing the vaccine."

Freddi approached the fridge and peered through the glass door. "The shelves are labelled." He looked closer. "The middle one says, um, 'P1-N5' I think. Yeah, P1-N5. That's what they all say."

I knew nothing about scientific classifications, but I recognised that code immediately. It was the name of the medical supplies that Patti was taking to Manupia.

"What's P1-N5?" said Freddi.

"It's the Fertillan plague," said Keya.

A line of terrifying, disparate dots suddenly joined up in my brain and I understood what had made Keya scream.

"We have to stop Patti." I ran out into the corridor.

"Stop Patti do what?" Freddi chased after me. "Cassy, wait!"

I had to stop at the exit to Section Five to activate the closed door. Fortunately, security clearance was only required to get in, not to get out. Freddi caught up with me.

"Stop Patti do what?" Freddi asked again.

"Take the plague to Manupia."

The door opened and I ran through to the next security door. I reached out for the control, but the door slid open of its own accord.

Behind it stood Prince James and at least two members of the Fertillan Guard that I recognised from his ship. All of them were in civilian dress.

I was so surprised, it took a split second for me to reach for my sidearm.

Time enough for the guardsmen to pull their EEWs first and aim them at me. I froze with my fingers mere centimetres from the grip of my gun. Close enough to sense it was there, but too far away to rip it from its holster without being shot.

"Hands up!" said one of the guardsmen.

A sickening feeling twisted my stomach. I raised my hands.

"You too!" came the order directed behind me and I knew that Freddi had also been too slow to reach for his weapon.

Prince James, dressed unusually casually in plain grey shirt and trousers, but still with the confidence of a man born into royalty, looked me up and down.

"Sesaan Cassandra," he said, eventually. "Why is it that everywhere I turn, I find you?"

"Perhaps you keep turning up in the wrong places," I said.

He dismissed my suggestion and glanced behind me. "With your little sidekick too. Isn't that an added bonus?"

James waved his hand as some sort of indication to his guards and one of them came and relieved me of my sidearm while the other kept their EEW squarely aimed at my chest. They took Freddi's sidearm too.

"Zelenski!" ordered James and a woman in civilian dress behind him snapped to attention. "Check Section Five for any other unexpected personnel."

"Sire," she said and ran ahead to where she would, no doubt, find Keya.

"What are you doing here?" I asked him.

He smiled innocently. "I've come to get my vaccine."

We were led back the way we had come into Section Five where we were corralled into the annexe next to the isolation room. Zelenski brought Keya at gunpoint to join us.

James followed her in and, behind him, came a man in scientist whites who I assumed to be a member of Leontes Station staff.

"What shall I do with you two?" said James.

It was a rhetorical question, but I answered it anyway. "You could let us go."

"Not one of the options I was considering," he said.

"If anything happens to me, you'll have Prince Stephen to answer to," I said.

James's face flared with anger. "You think because you are my brother's whore, it makes you somehow immune? Well, let me tell you, *whore*, that I don't answer to my brother. I answer to King Richard. The King who is my twin. We were born first while Stevie, unfortunately for him, came later which means he has less authority than he would like to pretend. So, let me assure you that I have no fear of answering to my younger brother if I have to."

Freddi cut in to change the subject. "What do you want with the vaccine?"

James raised his eyebrows in surprise. "The little sidekick speaks!"

"Vaccine?" said Keya. "The vaccine against the Fertillan plague? *My* vaccine?"

"Yeah," said Freddi. "That's what he said he'd come for."

Keya glared at James. "*You* were the anonymous client?"

"Not that I have to answer you," said James. "But, yes, I was the anonymous client who paid to develop a vaccine against the plague. Which works rather well, I'm told. So thank you very much. The trial data is excellent."

"But why?" said Freddi. "The plague died out on Fertilla."

"Or lies dormant," said James. "We need to be prepared in case it returns. The number of people who died in the original outbreak was, as I'm sure you know, quite considerable. Getting the economy back on its feet with such a gap in its working population was a gargantuan effort. Which, thanks to my family, we achieved."

The scientist cleared his throat. "I don't like to interrupt, Your Highness, but we *are* on a schedule."

"Yes, yes." James signalled to Zelenski and the guardsmen. "Put those three in the isolation room."

"What?" cried Keya.

I exchanged worried glances with Freddi.

"It'll keep you out of the way," said James.

"I can't go in there! The plague is in there!" cried Keya. "I'm not from Fertilla – I have no immunity!"

James smiled. "Then we shall vaccinate you."

He signalled to the scientist who disappeared out into the corridor while Keya continued to plead with James to no avail.

The scientist returned with a syringe in one hand and two biohazard suits thrown over one arm. "I can't imagine they'll walk in there willingly," he explained. "If you need to take them in at gunpoint, your staff will have to wear these to avoid contamination."

He dropped the yellow evi-plastic suits on the floor and pulled a little square packet from a pocket in his trousers. He tore the top off it with his teeth and I realised the packet contained a cleansing wipe.

Keya backed away from him until she hit the wall. "Don't do this, Maxiv, please."

It seemed the two scientists knew each other.

"It's perfectly safe, Doctor Sharma. We've virtually completed the last of our human trials. It's better than letting them shoot you."

"But you know as well as I do that a vaccine takes time to be effective. You can't give it to me one minute and the next minute throw me into an infected room."

"Hold out your arm, Doctor Sharma."

As if to give her extra encouragement, Zelenski lifted her EEW and pointed it at Keya.

She held out a shaky arm. The scientist took her wrist and held it steady. He pushed up her sleeve, cleansed the skin above her vein with the wipe and injected while she turned her head away.

Maxiv then left with James to, presumably, conduct whatever business they were there to conduct, and the guards ordered us into the decontamination chamber. I tried to think of a way to overcome three armed guards, negotiate a series of security doors and reach our ship so we could escape with our lives, but every possibility that I ran through my mind ended in all three of us being shot dead.

Mel was waiting on the other side. She broke into an enormous smile when she saw me. "Cassy! What took you so long? I thought you'd forgotten me."

Then she saw the suited, armed guards behind us and her excitement evaporated.

Three ration packs were thrown in after us and the guards backed out.

"Hey, Zelenski!" I called after them. "Do you know everyone hates crewing with you because you snore in your sleep?"

Zelenski, enveloped in protective evi-plastic, didn't so much as react. She and the other guard backed out and closed the door behind them. Its locks clicked into place and we were trapped.

"What was that about?" Freddi asked me.

"It was the only ammunition I had," I said.

Mel came up to us. "What's going on?"

Keya literally jumped back from her and skittered across to the other side of the room. "Keep away from me!"

Vendra stirred in her bed and coughed a weak and rasping cough. Kendov lay still, his laboured and wheezy breath clearly audible in the enclosed room.

"This is *bad*, Cassy," said Freddi.

I nodded. There was nothing else to say.

A voice came out over speakers hidden somewhere in the room. It took me a moment to realise it was James's voice. "Oh," he said. "Just to reassure you that you're not going to be shut in there forever, when I get home, I'll ask Stevie to come and fetch you."

Nothing else came over the speakers and I was left to calculate how long before Stephen could rescue us. With at least a day's travel in normal space at either end of the journey – even allowing for the possibility that James would send a message to his brother when he reached the Fertillan system rather than waiting until he got back to Londos House – we were talking more than three days. Assuming, of course, he went back to Fertilla straight away without going to Manupia first.

Three days stuck in a room with two people dying of plague, one vaccinated person, another possibly vaccinated person and the two of us relying on the immunity we had from previously being exposed to the virus…

Yeah, it was *bad*.

# Chapter Twenty Five

KENDOV WAS THE first to die. Vendra seemed to rally after that, but it was only for a few hours and then she suddenly took a turn for the worse and died soon after.

Mel remained uninfected.

Keya kept away from everyone else and huddled in the corner where she refused to touch anything, even one of the ration packs that had been left for us. I think she would have stopped breathing if she could have.

I sat with my back against the wall with the one-way glass in it – which looked black from the inside of the isolation room – and watched Freddi trying to break out of the door.

They had taken our guns, but they hadn't searched us and Freddi still had the knife he always carried around with him. It was useless to try to open a door sealed so completely that not even germs could escape and all he seemed to be able to do was scratch the door and the frame around it.

All of a sudden he let out an almighty yell and flung the knife so hard, it flew like a spear across the room. Mel ducked in panic, even though it didn't go anywhere near her head, and all of us watched as the point of the knife hit the glass. I hoped, for one desperate moment, that it would shatter the window and allow us to climb out. But we had already tried, and failed, to get out of the room that way. The window was made of supremely toughened glass and the knife didn't so much as scratch it. It landed on the floor an arm's reach from me.

"Try not to kill us with that thing before we get rescued," I said as Freddi came to retrieve his knife.

"But, if I asked you, you'd use it to kill me, wouldn't you, Cassy? If get the plague?"

"Don't talk drakh. We're immune. Keya found antibodies in our system."

"We're still going to be immune after three days locked up in here?"

"Yes!"

Keya, sitting across the room from us, stifled a cough.

Freddi shot me a worried look. "Virus or nerves?" he said, keeping his voice low.

"Nervous cough, definitely," I said. I hoped.

Freddi put his knife back into his inside jacket pocket and held out his hand. "Give me your P-tab."

"We've already tried that, this room is shielded, we can't get a signal out."

"Don't argue, Cassy, just give it to me."

I handed him my P-tab. At least if he was fiddling with that it would keep his mind off getting sick.

He then went over and asked Keya for her P-tab.

"Don't touch me!" she cried out.

Freddi kept his distance, asked her again, and she slid her P-tab across the floor towards him.

When he came back, Freddi had three P-tabs, including his own. He sat on the floor next to me, took out his knife and started to dismantle them.

"Do you think Patti knew she was taking the plague virus to Manupia?" I asked him.

"I'd like to believe she didn't," said Freddi.

Mel came over and sat on the floor with us. "What are you doing?" she asked Freddi.

But I was the one who replied. "He's making sure I need to buy myself a new P-tab when we get out of here."

"We will get out here, then?" she said.

"Of course." I tried to sound convincing.

"Do you think…" she began, then took a breath to compose herself. "Do you think all the people I helped get off Manupia were brought here and experimented on?"

I sighed. I hadn't dared think about it. "I don't know, Mel. Did you ever hear back from any of them?"

"At first, a few. But not for a while."

We allowed the thought to sit between us. It was an uncomfortable moment.

"Do you believe Prince James's story about developing a vaccine in case the plague comes back to Fertilla?" said Freddi.

"No," I said. "It's a nice cover story, but everything James has done has been about Manupia."

"Did you find out what he wants with Manupia?" said Mel.

I nodded. I was finally joining *all* of the dots and it was more horrific than I'd thought possible. "Are you sure you want to hear it?"

"You've just told me I've been helping to send people from my planet to suffer a horrible death, so yeah, I want to hear it."

I gathered my thoughts and started from the beginning. "We know that Manupia is a factory planet with a solid reputation, but it's old-fashioned and competitors are taking its business, meaning some of the factories have closed and made people workless. In order to compete, the factories are looking to automation. But if you replace people with machines, that means–"

"Even more people are workless," said Mel.

"The number of Manupians without jobs is already causing a problem. Could you imagine what would happen if thousands, maybe millions, of people became workless? There would be riots, chaos, anarchy. Unless you could get rid of the workers in some way."

Mel's eyes widened. She looked across at the corpses of the factory workers on their beds. She understood and, when she spoke, her mouth was so dry, she hardly made a sound. "The plague."

"By the Deity, Mel, I hope I'm wrong."

She leapt to her feet. "We have to get out of here." She banged on the glass. "Hey! Hey! Let us out! Let us out!"

Freddi let go of the knife, and the piece of P-tab he was fiddling with, and they dropped into his lap. "That's what Prince James meant when he talked about what happened on Fertilla. He couldn't stop himself boasting about how the royal family were able to get the economy on its feet again when so many people died."

"I'm thinking, Prince James and President Udinov already had a close relationship because he had done that deal with the coffee.

Udinov tells James about this problem he has with so many people likely to be made workless and they come up with a plan to get rid of them."

"Genocide?" said Freddi. "Can they really be that evil?"

"Why else would Patti be taking boxes of the plague virus to Manupia?"

"No," said Freddi. "I don't believe Patti would do that."

"She probably really thinks they are medical supplies. If you're going to have someone transport a biological weapon across the Rim, why not hire a former pirate and lie to her about it?"

"Then the vaccine…?"

"Is necessary to protect President Udinov and whoever else he wants to survive. Inoculate the key people, let loose the virus and wait."

Mel gave up hitting the glass, kicked the wall in frustration and went back to pacing the room.

A female voice suddenly came over the speakers. "–think I've found the intercom."

"Hello?" I called out. I jumped up and turned to the glass. "Hello? Is somebody there?"

"Cassy! Hello, can you hear me?" It was a male voice this time. "It's Stephen."

"Stephen?" Tears formed in my eyes. "Is it really you?"

If he answered, I didn't hear it because everyone in the room started shouting.

"Quiet! One at a time!" Stephen called over the speakers.

"How did you get here so quickly?" I said. I knew my estimate of a minimum of three days was accurate and we had been stuck in there for a day at the most.

"After your recent run-in with Corporal Louissi Eveshi, I decided to pull her off James's ship and question her about where James had been. Apart from Manupia, she told me he had come to Leontes a few times, so I brought her here with me on my ship."

"Hello, Cassy," said the female voice again and I recognised it as Louissi's.

"I knew Keya was on Leontes, so I thought I would speak to her about it," continued Stephen. "But when we arrived, no one knew where she was. That's when I got someone to check their internal security logs which said the last place she'd been–"

"For vac's sake!" Freddi interrupted, throwing the pieces of the dismantled P-tabs to the floor, now that his attempt to boost their signal was unnecessary. "Who gives a vac how you got here, just get us the vac out!"

# Chapter Twenty Six

E WAITED BY Patti's ship in the docking area of Shangi port on Manupia: Stephen, Mel and myself. Ironic that two of us had suffered so much to get off the planet and, less than a week later, we were right back where we started. At least the place was not crawling with Manupian security officials searching for me. Either they had given up or I had dropped way down their priority list. Even so, we had taken the precaution of travelling in Stephen's ship and bringing the shuttle down rather than take the risk of arriving in a ship registered in my name.

We heard Patti and Freddi talking before we saw them.

"I'm tired of Manupia," she was saying. "This is yesterday's world."

"Yes," said Freddi.

"Together, we could find somewhere that's moving forward into tomorrow, with more opportunities to do something different…"

She came round the side of an abandoned wheeled transport – her blond hair standing out, as ever, among the grime of the docking area – and stopped. The excitement on her face paled as she saw the three of us lined up in front of her.

"Freddi, what is this?" she said.

"We just want to talk, Patti," he said.

She gave him a betrayed look. "You never intended to take up my offer of crewing with me, did you?"

"No," he admitted.

"Can you let us in, Patti?" I asked her. "What we need to say to you should be said in private."

She regarded us all with suspicion. "This isn't a ruse to steal my ship?"

Stephen broke into laughter. "This ship?" He turned to look at its battered and carbon-smeared exterior.

"And who are you?" she said.

"I'm Prince Stephen Regellan of Fertilla," he said, giving her a little introductory bow.

She rolled her eyes. "Of course you are. The whole vacking planet's crawling with Fertillan princes."

"We're wasting time out here," said Freddi. "You need to let us in so we can talk."

She glared at him, angry that she'd been duped and, for a moment, I thought we were going to have to force her. But then she reached into her pocket, pulled out the remote control and opened the cargo bay doors.

As we all filed in, I looked around for the boxes of 'medical supplies' she had loaded up at Leontes, but the hold was empty. Mel and I sat down alongside one of the walls and I saw her body tremble as, like me, she remembered being locked inside for the journey to become human guinea pigs.

The others remained standing.

"Are you going to tell me what this is all about?" said Patti.

"What did you do with the medical supplies you brought from Leontes?" Freddi asked her.

"I delivered them."

It was the answer I was hoping she would not give. The tension from the others increased around me.

"What?" said Patti. "I got here yesterday. Do you think I would allow valuable cargo to sit around in my ship for a day while I'm not getting paid? I'm not that stupid."

"Where did you deliver it?" asked Freddi.

"Why should I tell you? If you want drugs, I can put you in touch with people who can get them for you, but I'm not giving you inside information so you can steal the ones I brought here."

Freddi looked across to me. "We need to tell her, Cassy."

"Can we trust her?" I said.

"At this point, we have to."

So I laid it all out for her. The whole, abhorrent plan to let loose a deadly plague to kill much of the population of Manupia.

She stared at me, with doubt in her eyes, through the whole story. She looked at Freddi, then Stephen and Mel.

"You all believe it, don't you?" she said.

"Believe it?" Mel leapt to her feet. "I lived it! You caged me in here and took me to a laboratory where they infected my friends and I had to sit with them while they died a hideous death. Now that's going to happen to everyone on this planet, except it's going to be a million times worse."

"You're blaming me for this?" retorted Patti.

Stephen stepped between the two women. "No one's blaming anyone," he said, looking in turn at each of them.

Mel scoffed and turned her back on him.

"The important thing," Stephen continued, "is that we find the plague virus and stop it being released into the population. Patti, you said you delivered it, where did you deliver it to?"

"Manupian security," she said. "I wasn't kidding about there being a black market in drugs. Medical supplies have a tendency to be stolen if they're not kept securely."

"So, what do we do?" said Freddi, looking at the others. "Because I don't want to be here when they let loose that virus, even if I do have some immunity."

"We should have some time," I said. "James had a maximum one day head start on us. If he was bringing the vaccine here, like we assume – and not going to Fertilla first, like he said – then it'll take time to vaccinate the great and the good, and then they'll need to allow time for the vaccine to become totally effective – maybe another day?"

"So," said Stephen, looking around at us all. "If you were going to poison a planet, how would you do it?"

"Environmental controls," I said, with a wave of dread at the thought of how easy it would be. "All the air, heat and lighting in all the cities is supplied through them. If I were twisted enough to want to unleash a virus into a city, I'd do it that way."

"I delivered those boxes to security here in Shangi city," said Patti. "If they're splitting them up to take them to the other cities, then they might not have left yet, which gives us a chance to stop them."

"So, you'll help us?" said Stephen.

"I don't know about that," said Patti.

"I can pay you if you like," he added. "I have the resources of a Fertillan prince, after all."

"Save a whole planet from a deadly plague and get paid for it?" She considered for a moment. "Sure, why not?"

# Chapter Twenty Seven

E STOOD AND waited for Patti around the corner from the Manupian security offices in Shangi city: Stephen, Freddi, Mel and myself. We must have looked conspicuous leaning up against the wall of a terraced house, but it was the middle of the working day and almost everyone was at the factories. Only one person walked past us and they were so used to ignoring workless on the streets, that they didn't even give us a second glance.

"We shouldn't have trusted her to go in alone," I said, as the waiting continued.

"You couldn't have gone in there," Stephen pointed out. "Less than a week ago, you were a wanted person as far as they were concerned."

"You or Freddi could have gone in there with her," I said.

"She's better off on her own," said Freddi. "She delivered the boxes on her own, she has to go in after them on her own."

Mel, I could tell, disliked the plan as much as I did and paced up and down with her hands in her pockets, saying nothing, but making her disagreement clear to everyone.

Eventually, Patti emerged from the Manupian security offices. Thankfully without bringing a troop of officials to arrest us, but also without any of the boxes.

"Well?" I asked, as she made it round the corner.

"The good news is, all the supplies meant for the other cities are still here," she said.

"You're sure?" I said.

"I checked them myself. I told them I'd lost a necklace of sentimental value that I thought might have fallen off into one of the boxes. So they let me go in and look at all the boxes loaded up ready to go out on the transports. It's dark out on the planet's surface, so they won't be leaving for several hours. I couldn't get them to say exactly when, but first light would be my guess."

"That's the good news," I said. "Which suggests there is also bad news."

"The shipment for Shangi city isn't there," said Patti. "I tried to get the guy to tell me where it was taken to, but he wouldn't say. He just said, if they found my necklace someone would probably hand it in and I could check back with him next week."

"What do we do?" said Stephen. "Even if I bring all the Fertillan Guard down from my ship, going into a Manupian security office with all guns blazing will be a blood bath."

"We attack the transports," I said. "Like the workless did to the car taking Prince James to Manupian Headquarters the first time I was here. They're vulnerable out on the planet's surface. The only thing is, we're going to need transports of our own to stop them."

"I can get those," said Mel, taking her hands out of her pockets and coming over to us. "We have a whole fleet of them in the Jonsonii factory. I know enough workers in the factory who will help me."

"What about the virus intended for Shangi city?" said Freddi.

"We have to assume it's been sent to the environmental control centre," I said. "Which means we have to get in there and stop it getting into the air supply."

"How are you planning to do that?" said Patti. "If you thought it was difficult for me to arrange for you to work in one of the factories, then you need to triple it to get into the environmental control centre. It's literally the lifeline for the whole city and it will be guarded."

"I don't know," I said. "But there must be a way."

THERE WERE NO signs, there was no visible security presence, there was nothing to suggest the large, locked, black door set into the wall at the edge of Shangi city near to the Jonsonii factory was in any way important. But Patti and Mel had both assured us that, behind it, lay the lungs of the city.

I waited down the street with Freddi. Mel had sourced us some dark brown boiler suits, which she thought would be a close match to the ones likely to be worn by the environmental centre workers. It was only the rucksacks on our backs, carrying all of our equipment, that were probably out of keeping.

"What are we going to do if this isn't where they took the virus?" said Freddi.

"This has to be the place," I said. "How else would you distribute an airborne virus other than through the air?"

Freddi peered out from the wall we were leaning on and looked further up the street for the umpteenth time. This time when he pulled back, there was a readiness in his eyes. "They're coming."

A mass of around twenty people were at the top of the street and running towards us. If Patti was among them, I couldn't see her within the throng of drably dressed people. They were the workless who used to shout at me outside the Jonsonii factory and they were rushing down the street because Patti had told them a lie that the environmental control centre was taking on employees.

Keeping myself close to the wall, I approached the entrance, with Freddi following close behind. The workless raced towards us from the other side and congregated around the door. I saw Patti in the crowd and she returned an acknowledging look before raising her fist into the air.

"Jobs! Jobs! Jobs!" she shouted, pumping her fist with every word.

Others joined in: "*Jobs! Jobs! Jobs!*"

The mob was excited, angry and desperate, but the door remained closed.

Patti pulled something from her pocket – a heavy metal clip from a cargo harness, I think – and chucked it at the door. It pinged uselessly to the ground, but it riled the mob.

"Let us in!" one of them cried.

"*Let us in! Let us in!*" mixed with cries of, "*Jobs! Jobs! Jobs!*" Until it was a mass of unintelligible shouting.

Someone opened the door a crack from inside and I readied myself.

A Manupian security official peered out warily with her EEW unholstered. The shouts subsided and she must have taken that as a sign it was safe to emerge.

This was our chance. We surged for the open door as the workless – either encouraged by Patti, or buoyed by their own fervour – surged with us.

The official fired an EE blast into the air. Some of the workless backed away from her warning shot, but most of them didn't care and we were carried on the wave of the crowd. The door was forced all the way open, the security official was pushed aside and we piled in.

I was physically propelled into the building. Freddi was virtually thrown forward into the back of me and we staggered off to the side as tens of workless spilled in behind us.

A paltry two Manupian security officials on guard unholstered their EEWs and pointed them at the crowd. Patti was no longer among them and must have withdrawn before they came into the building. But she had done her bit: the mob needed no further encouragement to be our distraction.

They filled what was a wide entranceway which seemed to serve no purpose other than to bridge the gap between the outer door and the inner sanctum of the building. The security officials had stepped forward from an ID-operated glass barrier at waist height which protected another security door on the other side.

One of the security officials tried to calm the crowd. "Quiet! Quiet!" He raised his hands in the air with his EEW pointing at the ceiling to defuse the tension. "What's all this about?"

"We were promised jobs!" shouted someone from the crowd, loud enough to be heard over the others.

"There are no jobs here," the security official foolishly replied. "The centre is fully–"

Anger erupted from the crowd. Someone must have picked up the harness clip which Patti had thrown at the door because it came sailing over the heads of the workless and struck the security official on the shoulder. He abandoned his passive stance and brought down his EEW as the crowd pushed forward and engulfed the officials.

I heard EE blasts and screams behind us as I ran to the glass barrier and vaulted over it. Freddi followed seconds behind me. The security team was too busy to even notice.

We got to the inner security door and, there, our incursion might have ended if it hadn't been opened from the inside. We hid behind the door as more security officials streamed out to help their colleagues deal with what was rapidly becoming a riot.

I caught the door before it closed again, slipped through, and we were both inside.

The plant was enormous, despite being about half the size of the Jonsonii factory floor. It was full of pipes strung from the ceiling and running along the walls, next to a maze of wire trunking and two giant metal tanks in the middle. The whole place hummed with electricity backed with the heavy rhythmic thump and release of air pumps again.

"Do you think they'll open fire on the crowd?" whispered Freddi, as we stepped further in.

"I hope not," I said, wishing there had been another way. "But a few wounded workless is better than a whole city dying from the plague."

Dotted around the plant were a few members of staff in grubby boiler suits similar to our own. In order to do what we had to do, they needed to leave.

Along the side wall, by an array of electric converters almost certainly connected to a solar array on the planet's surface, was bank after bank of control panels and, at the end of them, was the fire alarm. It was an old trick, but it was an effective one. I went straight over to it, lifted the protective cover and bashed the heel of my hand onto the button underneath.

The alarm wailed its obliging siren all around us, followed by several workers' groans as they realised they would have to evacuate.

I backed away from the alarm and hid with Freddi behind a large floor-to-ceiling pipe which ran up the nearside wall. The staff left with all the urgency of people who believe there's no fire and the alarm is part of a tedious exercise.

It wouldn't take long for them to realise it was a false, and possibly malicious alarm, so we had to work quickly.

"You look around," said Freddi as we emerged from behind the pipe. "I'll set the charges."

He headed to the far end of the plant, with his rucksack bouncing on his back as he ran, while I looked out into the vast space and evaluated the enormity of my task. I walked past the maze of pipes wondering how the vac I was going to be able to find the vials of plague virus in such a large area full of equipment. Assuming the vials were there and assuming they hadn't already been thrown into the air recycling system without leaving a trace.

One large tank dominated the centre of the room and had to be the main source of replenished oxygen which was pumped into the city. I put my hand on the cold, metallic surface and felt a slight vibration which told me it was in operation. If anyone was going to contaminate the air supply from the central source, then it was going to be linked in some way to that tank. It meant I could forget all the equipment that operated the heat, the lighting and other systems and concentrate my search around where I was standing.

That's when I saw a box like the one I had seen Patti load onto her ship, cast casually aside a few metres from the tank. As soon as I got near it, I could see it had been opened. I rummaged inside, but the only thing I found was the packaging which once held the vials.

Realising the vials were probably near by, I looked around again. This time, I looked above my head and that's when I saw a fat section of pipe which appeared to have been fixed between two thinner pieces. It was like the pipe had been broken and repaired using a fatter piece to join the two sections, with a sealing joint at either end, both of which had been welded solidly into place. The clean, almost shiny, piece of pipe appeared to be a recent addition, judging by the amount of dust and grime which coated all the other pipes.

Freddi jogged up to me. "I've set the charges," he said. "I hope it's going to be enough. There's no way to tell how thick the walls of this place are."

"It's going to need to be enough. I don't fancy trying to get out of here the same way we came in."

"Have you found the…?" he trailed off as he saw the box at my feet.

I kicked it out of the way. "It's empty."

"That means they definitely brought the virus here," said Freddi. "But what did they do with it?"

I pointed up at the bulging pipe. "What do you think?"

His gaze followed my finger, then traced the pipe back to where it was connected to the tank and, in the other direction to where it disappeared out through a wall. "Is that the pipe carrying oxygen into the city?"

"That's my guess."

"So, you're thinking the fat bit could be some sort of delivery mechanism?"

I nodded. "We need to take a look. Can you give me a lift up?"

Freddi obliged by interlocking his fingers so his hands formed a stirrup for me to step into. He hoisted me up and I grabbed hold of the thinner bit of pipe hoping it would be sturdy enough to bear my weight. I laid myself across it and pulled myself forward until I reached the new section. Set into it was a flat plate with a digital display which said *Valve Release* with a timer counting down from 01:05:34. Embedded beneath were the seals from the tops of six vials. The white stickers which had identified them as P1-N5 when they left Leontes had been taken off, but I was certain they were the same ones.

"Looks like we were right," I called down. "The vials containing the virus have been pushed into the pipe through some sort of device which stops them leaking out."

"If the virus has been plugged into system, then we're too late," said Freddi.

"I don't think so. There's a countdown to some sort of valve release." The display had changed to 01:05:33. At least it was counting down in minutes rather than seconds. "It's set for just over one day and five hours which would allow time for vaccinating whoever they want to survive."

"Then the virus is contained!" said Freddi. "All we need to do is remove that section of pipe and it won't be released into the city's oxygen supply."

The fire alarm abruptly stopped. Quiet seemed to rush in. Slowly, my ears adjusted to hear the electric hum of the station and the rhythmic sound of the air pumps.

We looked at each other and knew we suddenly had little time.

I pulled my EEW from where I had hidden it deep in my boiler suit pocket. "I'm going to cut through the thin piece of pipe on either side of the delivery mechanism to avoid disturbing the virus."

"Wait!" Freddi went over to the tank where a control panel was fixed to the side.

A computerised voice spoke from above. "Air replenishment system switched to maintenance mode."

"That's shut down the oxygen feed to the pipe," said Freddi.

I nodded as I realised I had narrowly avoided burning metal in the presence of pure oxygen and pulled the trigger on my EEW.

I fired in a continuous burst at a section of pipe on the far side of the bulge. Sparks flew off the metal and I had to turn away to avoid the risk of getting red hot splinters in my eyes. But the metal was thin and no match for an EEW. As the pipe cut through, I felt it vibrate where I was lying and I had to grab on tight to stop myself falling off.

"I can't hold it and cut the other side," I called down to Freddi. "Do you think you can catch it?"

Freddi had taken the breather out of his rucksack and strapped the canister to his waist. "Cassy, you need to put your breather on!"

"In a minute. Get ready to catch the pipe." I gave him no choice as I pushed myself back towards the tank and fired another continuous blast on the near side of the bulge. The pipe began to get hot with the heat generated by the gun and it was conducting along the metal to where I was holding on with my bare hand. I ignored it as much as I could until my skin felt like it was about to blister. I stopped firing for a moment to take off my rucksack which I dropped down to Freddi's waiting arms.

"Cassy, what are you doing?"

I ignored him as I unzipped the top of my boiler suit and pulled off the vest top I was wearing underneath. With the sleeves of my boiler suit hanging down, and in just my crop top bra from the waist up, I wrapped my vest around the pipe. The material wasn't the most effective heat barrier in the galaxy, but it was better than bare flesh. I resumed firing my EEW until the pipe – now almost entirely severed – bent under its own weight. It clung on by one last piece of metal which turned yellow, then red and suddenly gave way. Freddi side-stepped to catch the pipe with his sleeves pulled down over his hands. But it was still hot and he almost dropped the thing before he was able to safely lower it to the ground.

I slipped sideways off my precarious perch, but managed to grab two ends of my vest which was still wrapped around the pipe. It left me dangling with my feet less than a metre above the ground. Then I let go and dropped to the floor.

I grabbed my rucksack from where Freddi had put it and pulled out the breather I had brought with me. Freddi managed to put the cooling section of pipe into his own rucksack, but had barely thrown it onto his back when the door that we came through, inevitably, opened.

A Manupian security official, with his EEW drawn, stepped cautiously inside.

"Now, Freddi, now!" I urged.

Freddi reached into his pocket for the remote control he had hidden there and pressed its only button.

The boom of the explosion echoed around us and shock waves rumbled through the floor. The security official swung his EEW in panic and found the two of us in his sights. But we also had our EEWs drawn and both were aimed at him.

A siren more urgent and high pitched than the fire alarm screamed from above.

"Containment breach detected," said the same computerised voice which had announced maintenance mode. "All personnel evacuate. Sixty seconds to lock-in."

The security official glared at us with frightened eyes.

"You need to run," I told him. "The air in here is already being sucked out onto the planet."

But he kept his gun trained on me.

"All personnel evacuate," repeated the computer. "Fifty seconds to lock-in."

"You can pull the trigger," I said. "But you'll never shoot both of us before one of us shoots you."

"All personnel evacuate. Forty seconds to lock-in."

"If I turn my back," cried the increasingly nervous official, "how do I know you won't shoot me?"

"Because if I'd wanted to shoot you, you'd be dead already," I said.

"All personnel evacuate. Thirty seconds to lock-in."

"Cassy," urged Freddi. "We need to go."

The air was thinning. Not enough to make me gasp, but enough that I was taking increased breaths.

I backed away, keeping my gun trained on the hapless man. Freddi also backed away.

"All personnel evacuate. Twenty seconds to lock-in."

"Don't worry," I told the official as his breathing quickened. "Your city is safe. We've made sure of that."

I put my breather mask over my mouth and nose and took in the rich air.

"All personnel evacuate. Ten seconds to lock-in."

Panic gripped the official and he turned and ran for the door. I didn't see if he made it because both of us also turned and ran to the site of the explosion.

I heard the sound of the airtight blast doors close with finality and seal the room so the loss of atmosphere couldn't spread to the rest of the city. I hoped the man had enough time to reach the other side before the doors had shut.

Freddi's explosive charges had ripped a hole in the outer wall of the environmental control centre. Jagged pieces of double-skinned, insulated metal jutted out from the wound in its side. The breach was small, but enough to see the dusty, yellow surface of Manupia outside and enough for us to crawl through.

Freddi took off his rucksack and pushed it through first before he crawled after it. I got behind him on my hands and knees and felt a sharp piece of debris pierce the skin of my left palm as I picked my way through the opening.

We stood on the open plain of Manupia squinting into the sun that was pulling itself above the horizon many miles in front of us. I gasped at its sheer openness, but this time I didn't have

Stephen's hand to hold onto. All I had was the adrenaline pumping through my body that told me I needed to get away from the giant structure behind me that was Shangi city.

Freddi lifted an arm and waved. He grabbed my sleeve and pulled me forward. That's when I saw the white shape of a transport vehicle ahead of us and the long, black shadow it created as it was hit by the emerging sunbeams.

As we closed in on it, I could see Patti waving at us through the windscreen.

She disabled safety protocols to open the door of the climate-controlled cab and let us in.

We scrambled up next to her to share the generous passenger seat and removed our breather masks.

"Got what you wanted?" she asked.

Freddi tapped the rucksack on his lap. "Yep," he said.

She gave him a smile and we drove away.

<h1 style="text-align:center">CHAPTER TWENTY EIGHT</h1>

WE RACED ACROSS the plain of Manupia with Patti driving. She liked to drive fast and she didn't care what rocks or boulders we hit or how much we were bounced around in our seat. I clung onto any bit of the transport cab interior I could, to stop myself being totally knocked around and bruised, while Freddi protected the vials of virus in the pipe in his rucksack from any undue shocks.

We asked Patti to slow down and take it easy, of course, but she just laughed and kept going.

We skidded to a halt atop a shallow mound in the Manupian planet's surface. It was too small to be described as a hill, but it provided enough of a vantage point to see across the dusty, yellow plain beneath and the dark, metallic structure of Shangi city that we had just left.

Patti pointed towards the city. "We're in time. The transports have left Manupian security."

I looked again and, this time, I saw five plumes of yellow dust streaking out across the plain, all in different directions fanning out from a central point back in the city.

Another five plumes approached from three sides on an intercept course. They were travelling faster, creating large clouds of dust in their wake, which the strengthening sunlight lit up into a sparkling yellow haze. The transports near us were the first to intersect, quickly followed by the ones furthest from us and then the others in the middle. The clashing vehicles created a veil of dirt that made it difficult to see what was going on. But the debris soon settled and revealed the brown figures of Fertillan Guard in uniform out on the planet surface. As they crowded in on the transports which had fanned out from the city, figures in black Manupian security uniform emerged to confront them. It was like watching a ballet from the furthest seat in the theatre as the dancers carried out their moves to unheard music.

When the dancers stopped and the dust literally settled, Patti re-started the engine.

"It should be safe to approach now," said Patti and drove down the slope of the mound.

When we got there, two Fertillan Guards in breathers were holding two Manupian security officials at gunpoint. The man and a woman in black uniforms were on their knees with their hands on their heads; their anxious eyes staring out from over the top of their breather masks.

I put on my own breather mask and got out of the transport with Freddi. That's when I saw that one of the Fertillan Guards in uniform was Stephen. He called out to me, but his voice was lost in the thin air of the Manupian atmosphere. I pointed to my ear and made a shrugging movement to convey that I couldn't hear him.

When I got closer, he left the other guard to keep watch on the prisoners and turned to me. Our closeness enabled some of the vibrations of his voice to travel between us, while my rudimentary attempt at lip reading filled in the rest.

"Can you see if you can find the vials in the back of the Manupian transport?" he said.

"Okay," I replied.

As I spoke, some sort of aircraft flew across the sky above us.

"That's Louissi," said Stephen.

I looked up and recognised the shuttle from Stephen's ship as it landed some way from us, approximately in the middle of where all the transports had ended up.

Freddi had already clambered into the open cab door of the Manupian transport and released the locks that held the back section closed. So, when I got there, he was already moving around some of the boxes and bags to look for the vials. I climbed in to help him, but I hadn't even moved one thing before he stopped and looked at something down by his feet.

I stepped over to where he was standing and looking down at a very familiar box. I crouched, pulled at the flaps to break the seal and revealed a series of vials with little white stickers on the top which read 'P1-N5'.

I exchanged glances with Freddi and we knew we had stopped the plague virus getting out to another city. I hoped it was a scene being repeated in the other transports across the plain.

We carried the box out of the back and headed over towards Stephen. On the way, we saw Patti watching us from behind the windscreen of her transport. She held up Freddi's rucksack and beckoned him over through the glass. When he opened the passenger door and leant in to collect it, I sensed that something passed between them. Freddi had his back to me, so I couldn't see what he did or hear what they were saying, but he stayed long enough for it to be more than merely collecting a bag.

Freddi kept his face passive when he joined me again. He didn't so much as look back round as Patti started up the engine, spun her back wheels in the dust and headed back towards Shangi city.

Stephen gestured for the guardsman to take the box from my arms and carry it back to the transport they had used to intercept the Manupians. It left Stephen as the only one in charge of the prisoners. He raised his EEW and they flinched as they knelt, helpless, on the dust of the planet with their hands on their heads. He aimed his weapon not at them, but at their transport. He squeezed the trigger and an EE blast struck their nearside front tyre. It burst without resistance and the vehicle collapsed down onto the rim of its wheel.

With that, Stephen holstered his gun and strode off in the same direction as the guardsman.

It was only then that the Manupians realised they were being let go. Tentatively, they got off their knees. When no one tried to shoot them, they scrambled over to their handicapped transport. It would take them a while to sort out their tyre, but not longer than the air left in their breathers.

We joined Stephen in the transport he had used to intercept the Manupians. He was in the driver's seat, leaving me to squeeze onto the single passenger seat alongside Freddi. The guardsman was relegated to wearing his breather in the unpressurised rear compartment and looking after the box of vials.

Stephen's driving, although erratic, turned out to be less wayward than Patti's and we sped towards the rendezvous point without getting battered and bruised. Through the windscreen, I could see the dust trails of the other transports converging on where Louissi had landed the shuttle.

Four other transports arrived and four other boxes of vials were brought out of them. I was relieved to see all the ambushes had been successful, partly because they had had the element of surprise and partly because Stephen had been able to bring down a force of highly trained Fertillan Guard from his ship. There were just a few walking wounded, although one of the guardsmen had been seriously injured and had to be carried up the ramp into the gaping mouth of the shuttle's landing bay.

Mel was there. She jumped out of the cab of one of the other transports and ran over towards us. I opened the cab door and stepped down onto the planet's surface to greet her. With a big smile on her face, barely disguised by the breather mask covering it, she gave me an excited hug.

"Did you get the vials?" she said, her mask close enough for me to hear her words.

I nodded and glanced across to where the guardsman had got out of the back of the vehicle and was walking into the shuttle. She broke away from me and ran after him.

At the same time, Louissi came out wearing her own breather. She went straight over to Stephen and, with some urgency, said something to him that made his expression change from victorious to thoughtful. I went over and tapped him on the shoulder. He turned away from Louissi to me.

"What's going on?" I said, leaning into him so he could hear.

But it was Louissi who responded. Not that I could catch what she was saying. I had to mime to ask her to repeat. She started to, then gave up with frustration and urged all of us to go into the shuttle.

Freddi came up the ramp behind us and she hit the control to close the bay doors.

It was an interminable wait for them to shut, to form a seal and for the inside to begin to re-pressurise. But gradually, as the air poured in, I became aware of the groans of the seriously injured guardsman who was lying on the floor a couple of metres from me.

Louissi pulled down her mask. "Can you hear me now?" she said, looking around at Stephen, Freddi and me.

"Yes," I said.

The others nodded.

"I saw Prince James's ship on the flight over here," said Louissi. "It's on the ground not far from the Manupian Headquarters. If you want to catch him red-handed with the vaccine, Sire, this might be the opportunity."

"We need to destroy the plague virus first," said Mel, coming over to us. "Did you get the vials from Shangi?"

"I've got them here," said Freddi, pulling off his rucksack and clasping it in front of him.

Mel held out her hand. "Give them to me."

"No," said Stephen. "We take them off Manupia, jettison them out of an airlock and fire them into the sun."

"Too risky," said Mel. "We destroy them here, right now, where I can be sure it's been done. What happens if you're stopped by Manupian security before you leave the planet?"

"The factory worker has a point, Sire," said Louissi. "If the Manupian security officials didn't manage to send a message when they were first attacked, they will have done so now you've let them go. Reinforcements are very likely on their way. For the safety of your crew, Sire, I need to get them off the planet and back to the ship. We should be able to plead some diplomatic privileges under the Fertillan royal seal, but the Manupians will be within their rights to search the shuttle before letting us into orbit. If you want to be sure the virus doesn't get back into the hands of the Manupians, I would respectfully suggest you destroy it here if you can."

"You make a compelling argument, Corporal," said Stephen and nodded to Freddi.

Freddi relinquished his rucksack to Mel's unwavering outstretched hand.

"I will need the box that your man in uniform brought in here as well," said Mel. "I keep asking him, but he won't give it to me."

"Guardsman!" bellowed Stephen. "Give her the box."

Mel swung Freddi's rucksack over her back and took the box of vials from the sheepish guardsman standing at the back of the bay. She walked straight past Louissi and hit the control to re-open the door without so much as asking permission.

"Corporal," said Stephen to Louissi, shouting as the seals of the door released and the air began to dissipate once more. "I'm going to go after my vac-arse brother. Are you sure you're okay to get my crew back to the ship?"

"Yes, Sire. I'll try to create a bit of a diversion for you on the way out."

He said something else to her, but it was lost along with the atmosphere we had been breathing as it was sucked out through the door.

We all returned our masks to our faces while some of us prepared to step back out on the planet's surface.

# CHAPTER TWENTY NINE

MEL AND THE other factory workers who had driven to the rendezvous point put the boxes of vials and the pipe we had brought from the environmental control centre into the pressurised cab of one of the transports, along with some flammable material which looked like a few old bed sheets. Into the footwell of the cab they put two breather units with the valves of the masks forced open so they released a steady stream of air to keep oxygen flowing in the cab, even if the internal climate controls were destroyed.

In the silence of the thin atmosphere, Mel gestured for Stephen to hand over his EEW.

He must have realised what she was about to do because he unholstered his weapon and handed it to her without protest.

Mel opened the door to the cab enough to poke through the barrel of Stephen's gun. She fired a short burst onto the material and a solitary, embryonic flame flickered to life.

She closed the cab door, stepped back and we watched the fire dance through the glass of the windscreen. Soon, the whole cab was a mass of yellow and orange heat, bending and twisting within its prison as the vials inside were heated to a temperature that the virus couldn't survive.

Stephen stepped close to Mel and touched her arm to retrieve his EEW. She didn't turn to look at him as she handed it over; her gaze remained fixed on the inferno she had created.

The other factory workers who Mel had called upon to drive the transports must have decided they had seen enough because they started their engines and drove off in three plumes of dust.

Stephen got into the driver's seat of the final, surviving transport, while Freddi and I pulled Mel away from where she had continued to stand and watch the fire.

Somehow, the three of us – Mel, Freddi and myself – squeezed onto the passenger seat meant for one and we drove off to the Manupian headquarters.

WE COULD HAVE driven all the way to the Manupian headquarters and been shut out. We had no army, we had no way of breaking down the doors and they could have easily turned us away.

But Stephen was expert over the communicator. He stated that he was Prince Stephen Regellan of the Fertillan royal family and he had come to join his brother in a meeting with President Udinov – and he said it in such a way that it gave very little room for his request to be rejected. The polite, but somewhat confused voice on the other end thought about it, supposedly went away and checked with someone else, and then let us in.

Inside the building, we were met by a complement of five armed Manupian security officials in their black uniforms. At gunpoint, they ordered us to exit the transport with our hands raised. They took our EEWs from us and then passed a hand-held metal detector over us which was when they found, and confiscated, Freddi's knife.

After that, we were marched – again at gunpoint – down the wide, opulent hallways of the headquarters until we reached the double doors with two Fertillan Guards from James's ship standing outside. They did not seem concerned to see us, and I had to believe we were expected, as they continued to stare ahead while standing at ease.

One of the security officials knocked on one of the doors and listened for a reply. The doors were opened and we were taken inside.

The room was much like Stephen's ostentatious sitting room back at Londos House, except much grander and with a high ceiling that gave it a spacious feel. Drapes of finely embroidered material hung down from the back wall, while large family portraits dominated the walls at either side. It had no comfortable sofas, but imposing tall-backed armchairs covered in plush, maroon velvet, each with an ornately carved side table of real wood which sat upon a beige carpet that felt spongey underfoot. Sitting on five of the chairs was President Udinov, his two daughters, Maxiv the scientist who had vaccinated Keya at Leontes Station and Prince James. They all had a small cup and saucer perched on the table beside them which contained, judging by the smell which percolated through the room, fresh coffee. I wondered if they were drinking the undrugged stuff.

We – Stephen, Freddi, Mel and myself – remained standing by the door while the security officials fanned out behind and either side of us.

"Stevie." Prince James got to his feet. "How rude of you to join us."

"What the vac are you doing, James?" said Stephen.

"It's always delightful to see you, brother," said James, in a way that suggested entirely the opposite. "But this really could have waited until I returned to Fertilla."

"It really couldn't," said Stephen.

"President Udinov," said James, bowing politely towards his host. "May I introduce my extremely annoying *younger* brother, Stephen; my extremely annoying younger brother's whore–"

I felt myself recoil at his description of me as he pointed his index finger in my direction.

"–the whore's sidekick; and some woman I have never met before."

"My name is Melarny Frankinov," said Mel loudly and defiantly. "I'm one of the factory workers you planned to put to death by unleashing the plague."

Udinov flushed red and stood from his chair. "I don't know who's been feeding you these scurrilous rumours, Individual Frankinov, but they are categorically untrue. There *is* a threat of a new illness being brought to Manupia from outside, but we are making attempts to combat it. This man here is a scientist from the prestigious Leontes Station and brings with him a vaccine which we hope will protect everyone." He looked across to Maxiv, who seemed rather startled to be singled out, and put down his coffee. "In fact, I have chosen my family to receive this vaccine first in a demonstration of confidence in its effectiveness and safety. Sophea, you can take your vaccine now."

One of the young women, dressed beautifully in a long flowing dress with her natural blond hair draped across her shoulders, stiffened in her seat. "Now? In front of these people."

"I said we would do this tonight, Sophea, after coffee," said Udinov. "I think we have almost finished our drinks, haven't we?"

He addressed his question to Maxiv who nodded under duress and, as Udinov continued to stare at him, reached to the side of his chair where he had a small medical bag.

"James, why?" said Stephen.

In front of us, Sophea rolled up the sleeve of her dress at the same time as her face turned as pale as her hair.

"Because of the power it could bring us," said James. "Think of it, Stevie. The most powerful manufacturing planet in the Obsidian Rim aligned with the major food producer of the region. Sharing ideas, efficiencies, contacts."

"But to kill millions of people, James," said Stephen. "It's evil… it's inhuman."

"You should be careful what you accuse me of, Stevie. We're talking about a planet where millions of people are at risk of being made workless. It's going to happen whether the planet is brought to ruin through outside competition or it is forced to automate. For those people, destitute with no money for food, there is no life."

Behind me, I swear I heard at least one of the Manupian security officials shift uncomfortably. Everybody else in that room knew the truth behind what James and Udinov had been planning, with the possible exception of Udinov's daughters, but the security officials were almost certainly getting a hint of it for the first time.

"Ow!" protested Sophea as Maxiv's needle went into a vein in her arm.

"Sorry," he whispered. He was kneeling beside her, pushing the contents of a small syringe into her bloodstream. "Nearly done."

Stephen approached his brother and stood defiantly in front of him. Even though the heel of James's shoes made him taller, it was Stephen who had the moral superiority. "It won't work," said Stephen. "We have intercepted all the supplies of the plague you had brought to this planet."

"I did no such thing," said James.

"Maybe you paid someone who paid someone who – somewhere down the line – paid an ex-pirate to bring the vials here under the guise of medical supplies. Maybe you made sure the chain can never be traced back to you. But I *know* it was you, James."

James reached for his sidearm. The five Manupian security officials reached for theirs.

James pointed his gun squarely at his brother's head. Five other EEWs were suddenly trained on all of us.

Stephen raised his hands and backed away from his brother's gun. "I'm unarmed," he said. "You wouldn't shoot your own brother, would you?"

"I might," said James. "Given the right circumstances."

I glanced across at Freddi and I saw my own uncertainty reflected in his eyes as we also backed away. A feeling of regret twisted in my stomach as I wondered what harm it really would have done to let James continue with the vaccinations unhindered.

"It doesn't matter if you shoot us or you don't shoot us," said Mel. "Once we leave here, what's to stop you making more plague virus and carrying out your plan anyway?"

"I don't have to listen to this!" declared Udinov. "Letting your brother up here was a mistake." He waved across to the security officials who were between us and the door. "Arrest these four and keep them under armed guard."

The officials took a step forward. I glanced across at Freddi as we both raised our hands. But one of Mel's hands was reaching inside her cleavage. She drew out something long and thin and I saw that it was a sealed vial with a white sticker on top. I knew instantly what it was. So did half the other people in the room and their gasps were audible.

"By the Deity!" I said under my breath.

"Stop! All of you!" she said.

Everyone stared at the vial in her hand. The officials looked confused. They held their positions with their weapons aimed at us, but did not advance. It was then I realised that Mel had, somehow, skilfully manoeuvred herself so we stood between her and the people with guns.

"Mel," said Freddi. "Where did you get that?"

"I took a vial of plague virus from one of the boxes before we destroyed them all," she said. "As my insurance policy."

"Liar!" shouted Udinov. "It's a lie!"

"If you want to check if I am lying, you just need to read what the label says. It says 'P1-N5'." She looked pointedly at Maxiv who was sitting on the floor clutching his medical bag to his chest. "You know what that means, don't you?"

"It's the scientific code for the Fertillan plague," he confirmed.

She put one hand on the seal at the top like she was ready to pull it off.

"Shoot her! Shoot her!" screamed Udinov.

The security officials looked confused for a split second as they realised Freddi, Stephen and I were all in their line of fire. But they readied their guns to shoot anyway. The three of us dived for cover and hit the floor as Mel unsealed the vial and threw it over President Udinov.

He screamed.

Five EE blasts streaked from the officials' weapons – four of them struck Mel in the chest and the fifth hit the drape on the wall behind. The force of the blasts sent Mel's body flying backwards and she was almost certainly dead before she hit the floor.

Udinov's continued screams relayed a terror that I had never heard before. He kept wiping his face with the sleeve of his jacket while holding out his other arm to the petrified scientist. "Vaccinate me! Vaccinate me!" His screams coalesced into terrified words.

The whole room was madness. Udinov's daughters had jumped from their seats. One of them was screaming almost as loud as her father. The other one, Sophea, kept saying to no one in particular, "Is it true? Is it true?"

The EE blast which had hit the drape had caused a smouldering burn which ignited into a flame.

The two Fertillan Guards had rushed in from their sentry duty and kept switching the aim of their EEWs from one Manupian security official to the other to cover the room. None of them seemed to know who the enemy was. Perhaps because the enemy was a microscopic virus which Mel had set free when she opened the vial.

I scrambled to my feet. "We have to get out before we're all exposed!" I yelled above the chaos.

Freddi and Stephen were also on their feet, but five terrified Manupian security officials and two confused Fertillan Guards still had their weapons drawn and stood between us and the door.

James also held his weapon, but it hung loosely at his side. "Did she really have the virus?" he asked Stephen.

"She was willing to be killed to throw it in Udinov's face, so yeah," said Stephen. "I think she really had the virus."

Something snapped in James like he suddenly understood what was going on. "Everybody out!" he yelled. "Now! Now! Now!"

The Fertillan Guards were first to obey. The Manupian security officials seemed to pick up on the sense of panic and ran after them. With weapons no longer pointed at us, we were finally able to get out into the hallway with Udinov's daughters and Maxiv close behind us.

James was the last to leave and stood looking back from the doorway as Udinov staggered away from the fire which was leaping up the drape. He looked totally disorientated with his eyes bloodshot from the either the plague virus or his desperate attempts to rub his eyeballs clean.

James didn't step back to allow him through. Instead, he lifted his EEW and pointed it at Udinov. "You're infected, you can't come out," he said.

"But James," said Udinov in disbelief. "I'm the President."

"I'm told the plague is a terrible way to die," said James. "It's a kindness if you don't suffer."

An EE blast shot out of the end of James's gun and hit Udinov in the forehead.

Blood sprayed from the wound and his lifeless body collapsed to the floor.

Udinov's daughters screamed.

James came out into the hallway and closed the doors behind him as the sirens of a fire alarm wailed around us. This time, triggered by a real fire.

# Chapter Thirty

LOOKED AT MYSELF in the mirror on the back of Stephen's wardrobe door and saw a woman who wasn't me.

The dress followed the curves of my body as it draped in folds of shimmering blue from the low neckline, across my breasts, in tight at the waist and flared in folds that stretched down to my ankles. My hair had been washed and brushed until it shone and was twisted so it lay in a neat, single braid across the front of my right shoulder. One of the women in Londos House had tried to put make-up on my face, but I hated the way it clogged up my skin and put false colour on my cheeks and so I had washed it off again.

Even without the make-up, my reflection reminded me of how Udinov's daughters had looked in the minutes before their father was infected with the plague virus and then shot dead in front of them. It brought back the memory of how they acted afterwards.

One of the daughters had been unable to cope and ran screaming up and down the corridors in hysterics. The reaction of the other one, Sophea, had been completely the opposite. She had put aside her terror and grief and taken charge. She let the fire alarm seal the room where Mel had released the plague, but stopped the automatic systems from venting the atmosphere so the fire could consume the whole room and kill the virus. She completely locked down the headquarters and prevented anyone from leaving in case they had been contaminated and carried the plague to other parts of Manupia. That included us. Stephen, James, Freddi and me were forced to wait it out in a transport until quarantine was lifted. It was during that time that the two princes enacted a truce and promised not to kill each other.

In the mirror, I saw Stephen come up behind me. He placed his chin on my shoulder and put an arm around my waist so I felt the smoothness of his newly shaved skin nuzzle into my neck and his embrace draw me into his body.

"You look amazing," he said into my ear.

"I feel over-dressed," I said.

"That's the idea of a party," said Stephen. "It gives you the chance to dress up."

"Will it be enough to impress your mother?"

"I'm hoping that *you* will be enough to impress my mother. But I think the dress will help."

He spun me around on the spot so I turned away from our reflection and I was looking into his real eyes. They were gentle, loving and made me want to kiss him. My lips caressed his lips and warmth tingled through my body. I wanted to take off the dress, strip him of his elegant black suit and white shirt and return to the bed in which we had lain only hours before. But I knew we had no time, that somewhere else in

Londos House the party had already started, and I had promised I would attend.

As our lips parted, I thought how much more difficult kissing would have been if I had been wearing the lipstick the woman from the royal staff had wanted me to wear. I broke into a childish giggle.

"What?" said Stephen.

"Doesn't matter," I said.

"Tell me what's so funny."

I shook the thought from my mind and composed myself. "Come on, let's get going."

I took Stephen by the hand and led him out into the corridor. From there, he took over as I didn't know where we were going, and we went down several passageways to a room I hadn't been in before.

It was stunning. Like the room at the Manupian headquarters, it had a high ceiling and drapes of fabric which adorned the walls. It wasn't lit by ambient lighting like I was used to experiencing on planets, asteroids and space stations, but a single fixture of sparkling cut glass that hung down from the ceiling and sent out rays of warm light in all directions. It was almost devoid of furniture, apart from a few tall, cushioned stools to perch upon around the sides and one, single upright armchair where a very old woman was sitting attended to by a male member of staff.

There were up to twenty people milling around, most of them dressed in finery to rival my dress and Stephen's suit, casually chatting to create a gentle murmur which mingled with the sounds of soft music playing from hidden speakers. There were a few people dressed more conservatively and I concluded they were members of household staff. One of them offered me a tall, thin glass of pale yellow liquid which I took from them out of curiosity. Stephen was also given a glass, from which he took a perfunctory sip. I sniffed at my drink and detected the tang of alcohol, but when I tasted it, it was strangely bitter and nothing like beer. So I took to holding it as some sort of accessory, which many of the other guests also seemed to be doing.

"You should be careful of those drapes," I said to Stephen as we went further into the room. "They could be a fire risk."

He chuckled. "I think the idea is that we avoid weapons fire in here."

I smiled and tried to settle my nerves as Stephen steered me towards a man with a full, but neatly trimmed, brown beard who was holding hands with a tall, skinny woman. I recognised him immediately as King Richard. The family resemblance was clear in the shape of his wide Regellan nose, dark brown hair and blue eyes, but if someone had asked me to guess which of his brothers was his twin, I wouldn't have been able to say. I could see traces of both Stephen and James in him, although his choice to grow a beard clearly set him apart.

"Richard," said Stephen. "I would like you to meet Sesaan Cassandra."

I attempted to curtsey like I had been taught on my first visit to Londos House and wobbled a little bit in the delicate shoes I had been given to wear.

When I brought myself to standing tall again, I realised Richard was looking me up and down like he might do to an object in a shop that he was considering for purchase.

"Do you love her, Stephen?" said Richard, once he had seen enough.

"I do," said Stephen.

"Then, good." King Richard smiled. "Have you met Triana?"

The tall, thin woman turned to Stephen, uncoupled her hand from the King and curtsied.

There followed an exchange of bowing, curtsying and shaking of hands as everyone was introduced to everyone else.

"I'm think of marrying her next year and starting a family," said Richard, conspiratorially. "That will really put James's nose out of joint."

"Congratulations," said Stephen.

Richard drank the rest of the pale yellow liquid in his glass and took Triana with him as he went to find a member of staff for a top-up.

"That went well," said Stephen.

"It did?" I said.

"Oh, yes."

"What did he mean by, 'put James's nose out of joint'?"

"At the moment, James is next in line to the throne. But as soon as Richard has children, the line of succession passes to them."

"Even when they're a baby?"

"Oh, yes."

We mingled a little more and were unable to avoid encountering James who regarded us both with a superior look.

"Stevie," he said in his usual condescending manner. "I see you have with you–"

"My name is Cassy," I said, before he could use his favourite insult.

"Of course it is," said James. "Delightful party, isn't it?"

"Delightful," agreed Stephen.

The two brothers parted company, but the tension they generated remained between them across the crowded room.

In the days we had sat waiting it out in the transport at the Manupian headquarters, the princes had agreed a plan of action that they said would safeguard them all from recriminations. Stephen would not mention James's dealings with Udinov and James would not involve himself in Stephen's business. I thought it was a poor bargain, as James's actions would have been nothing less than a war crime, if we had been at war. In a time of peace, they represented conspiracy to mass murder at a level that went beyond criminality. But it was a deal they needed to keep if they were also to prevent trouble for Sophea and the Manupians. She agreed to keep quiet about James's execution of her father. She concocted a story to say that Udinov had become very sick and, in his delusion, accidentally started a fire at their home in which he burnt to death. If both the princes played their part and didn't reveal the plan to infect Manupia with the plague, then scandal would be avoided and the apparent integrity of both ruling families would remain intact.

It was a dirty pact, but in an imperfect galaxy, I accepted it was necessary. For the time being, at least.

With the tension between the brothers starting to dissipate in the room, Stephen took me to meet his mother.

She was the old woman I had seen earlier sitting in the only proper chair in the entire room. She was dressed in the same type of shiny material as my dress, but hers was black and buttoned up right under her chin, and with sleeves which ran the length of her arms to her bony wrists. Three beaded necklaces of tiny coloured spheres hung down over her modest bust and amounted to her only adornment. Her hair had passed beyond grey to be white and was pulled back into a bun at the back of her head, which did something to tighten the skin of her face which had loosened into wrinkles over the years.

"Mother," said Stephen, bowing towards her with respect. "I would like you to meet Sesaan Cassandra."

I curtsied and the woman glared out at me from the confines of her chair. "Isabette?" she said.

"No, Isabette was my mother," I said. "I am Sesaan Cassandra, but people call me Cassy."

"You're *dead*!" she said.

I looked up to Stephen for help.

"It's okay," he said. "She gets a little confused sometimes."

"In the fire! You died in the fire!"

"That was my mother," I said.

"Have you come to haunt me, Isabette?"

"I'm not Isabette." I stepped back from the increasingly agitated woman.

Members of the royal staff fussed around her. The one who had been attending to her earlier took hold of her wrist to take a pulse, but she shook her arm free.

"You bitch! You whore!" She pulled herself to her feet – frail as she was – and pointed an accusing, bony finger at me. "You slept with my husband behind my back! You deserved to die! Go ahead and haunt me, Ghost Isabette, because I have no regrets about setting fire to your house – and given half the chance, I'd do it all over again."

The horror of the revelation took my breath away. It claimed my blood. I felt the colour drain from my skin and retreat inside of me.

Members of staff hushed her and pulled her back into her chair.

Stephen approached me. "She's an old woman, she doesn't know what she's saying."

But I flinched from his outstretched hand.

I turned and ran. Other party guests stared and clasped their delicate glasses of pale yellow alcohol as they parted to get out of my way.

I heard Stephen's voice calling: "Cassy! Cassy!" But I ignored him.

I hurried out the door and my ankle twisted as I tried to turn in the corridor in the stupid shoes I had been given to wear. I kicked them off and ran in bare feet, down the corridors of Londos House and out into the street.

FREDDI FOUND ME.

It might have been many hours later, I wasn't sure.

I stood in the street outside the offices of Edsom's Exporters and stared at the building that had replaced the house where my mother had once lived.

Where my mother had once died.

Freddi touched my shoulder. I didn't flinch. I had sensed he had been standing next to me for a while. He was the only one in the street who didn't stare at me as I stood, sweaty from running, in a shimmering blue dress and bloodied, naked feet.

"How did you find me?" I said.

"Stephen messaged me," said Freddi.

"He didn't have the guts to come himself?"

"He said he thought you might not be receptive. He also thought a prince coming to the street might attract attention. Although, in that dress, you seem to be doing quite well with that on your own."

We stopped speaking for a while. I kept staring at the building.

"They killed her, you know," I said.

"Who?" said Freddi.

The answer was obvious. Too horribly, hideously obvious. "That's what James meant when he said that I should think about what happened to my mother. All those years ago, when I was a child, her relationship with King John became too close. It angered his wife and so she had her killed."

"You can't be sure of that, Cassy."

"I can." The way Stephen's mother, the widow of King John, had looked at me, I knew my face had sparked recognition inside of her. People who had seen the old photographs of my mother often said how much I looked like Isabette.

"It all makes sense now," I said. "The reason I was staying over at a friend's place that night wasn't a coincidence. Someone did it on purpose to get me out of the way before they set fire to the house."

"I'm sorry," said Freddi.

"And now I'm doing it all over again, aren't I?" I fought back my tears of anger, grief and self-loathing. "I'm repeating my mother's mistakes. I've fallen for the charms of a member of the Fertillan royal family and look where it's brought me. Right back to where my mother died. It's an omen, Freddi. I need to break out of the cycle."

"But you love Stephen," he said.

"I am a lowly, freelance spaceship captain. I have no right to love a prince."

"Perhaps we should get you away from Fertilla for a while," he suggested.

"Yes."

"Wormhole out of the system, find some disgusting asteroid or space station and take a safe, boring freelance job like we used to."

"Yes. We should go back to the ship."

I turned to walk away, but pain shot through both my feet and I cried out.

"Are you okay?" he asked.

"I came out without any shoes."

Freddi made me sit down on the step of Edsom's Exporters and lift up my dress a few centimetres so he could look at my feet. He winced at the bloodied mess. Then he began picking pieces of grit off the soles of my feet and wiping down the blood as best he could. Finally, he took off his own shoes and put them on me.

He helped me to stand and I felt the pain again, but much less this time. I took a tentative step forward. It hurt, but not nearly so much and I was able to walk along the street while leaning on his shoulder, even if his shoes were a bit too big for me.

"Freddi," I said as we walked. "For a relatively short man, you have surprisingly large feet."

"Thank you, Cassy," he said. "I'll take that as a compliment."

* * *

Sign up to my newsletter to receive updates on all my latest
releases:
janekillick.com/newsletter

# ASSASSIN
# FREELANCER BOOK THREE

*Framed for an assassination she didn't commit, Cassy must prove her innocence to bring a life-saving technology back home.*

When Freelance spaceship captain Cassy discovers an assassin at the wedding of her ex-lover, Prince Stephen, she fights to wrench his rifle away. But a stray blast shoots into the royal party and kills Queen Triana. Knocked unconscious, Cassy wakes to find herself holding the murder weapon, the assassin gone and a squad of guards who condemn her as guilty.

Can Cassy find the real assassin and prove her innocence? Can she find the lost spaceship and bring back its secrets? Can Cassy and Stephen ever be together?

*Find out in* Assassin, *the page-turning conclusion to* The Freelancer Trilogy